HEROINES

AN ANTHOLOGY OF SHORT FICTION AND POETRY

VOLUME 4

Sarah Nicholson
Editor

I0589702

Lore White
Contributing Editor

THE NEO PERENNIAL PRESS

Published by The Neo Perennial Press
Wollongong, Australia.
www.theneoperennialpress.com

Cover design: Tim Donnelly

National Library of Australia Cataloguing-in-Publication entry
Creator: Sarah Nicholson
Title: Heroines: An anthology of short fiction and poetry. Volume
4/Edited by Sarah Nicholson
ISBN: 978-0-9946453-4-0
Subjects: Women--Fiction. Mythology. Fairytale. Folklore.

CONTENTS

Delia
Wes Lee

When you clean someone's house it doesn't seem real like your
own. It's like a museum display where the things don't move and
have no real meaning. No memories in the rooms, of lying in the
bath, or standing in the kitchen when something terrible
happened, picking up the phone and hearing the unimaginable,
there's none of that. No corners to surprise you, where you
remember a conversation or a fight. Ornaments don't mean
anything — who gave you what and where it was from —
nothing rises in you when you touch them, no energy burning off.
Things don't speak, they're silent. I liked the silence. I liked being
in that calm little world.

I told her my name was Delia. That I was an experienced cleaner.
I handed her the reference I'd written the night before. She sized
me up through thick, false eyelashes.
"It's been a mission," she said as she led me through the house.
"Finding someone local, you wouldn't believe what we've been
through."
Wall-to-wall, cream shagpile throughout. Silver wallpaper
embossed with a black velvet flower pattern. The rooms large and
full of shadows.
"You'll find everything you need in here." She opened a
cupboard in the kitchen. "We're never home before 7pm, you
know what the traffic's like. Peter's in real estate, and I own a
gallery in town. Cornucopia, do you know it?"
"Yes," I told her.
Italian lamps in convoluted shapes. Low light, high light, lights
highlighting paintings along hallways that led to bathrooms and
bedrooms and guest rooms. Paintings everywhere like a castle. A
small envelope with cash left out for me on her dressing table in
the bedroom, propped against a blue glass ornament. Delia
written on it in her flowing handwriting. Sometimes she'd leave a
note folded in with the bills thanking me for something extra that

she'd noticed. His side of the bed and hers. Clutter on the bedside tables, books piled high that never changed their position. Soiled tissues in the wastepaper basket. Wet towels dropped on the floor in the bathroom. Cotton balls on the vanity smeared with moisturiser and foundation. I liked looking through their things, their contraceptives in her top drawer. The way they hung their clothes, colour-coordinated in the wardrobe. The framed photos on the piano. Her false eyelashes peeled off in plastic containers, unhinged on their settings, carelessly plonked down. I smelled his aftershave in the bathroom, lingering in the air hours after he'd left. Cigarette smoke on his clothes hanging in the wardrobe. There were no ashtrays. I imagined him smoking in his car, a furtive thing, or just something she couldn't stop, something he didn't bring home, something he kept for himself.

When I arrived in the morning I'd light a cigarette, sit on the balcony and stare out over the rocky shoreline. The mist slowly lifting, revealing shallow pools of water if the tide was out. The rock eroded away in smooth, protruding shapes like the red sandstone cliffs I'd seen in photos of the Mediterranean. I remembered watching Death Takes a Holiday when I was a teenager. Fredric March as Death, deciding he wanted to feel what it was like to be human. Visiting the world in the guise of an Italian count. Lounging on a stone balcony somewhere on the Amalfi coast, smoking a cigar in a crisp white suit, tired of bringing havoc to the world. There was something about Death wearing a pencil moustache and a white linen suit, swirling an olive in a dry martini. He was so urbane. He longed for the same things as we all did, a holiday, a rest.

I'd stare out to sea and breathe in deeply, trying not to think about arriving home. Malcolm's note still on the fridge under a magnetic hippopotamus, its purple mouth grinning: Just nipped out to get some basil, back in 20, bottle of wine in the fridge. Love you hon. So casual, so breezy, so filled with the night he'd planned for us both. And I thought, if Death could take a holiday why couldn't I take a holiday from death?

I'd fill a bucket in the kitchen sink with hot soapy water, squeeze out the mop and start in the bathrooms. Scrubbing the bath, making great wide circles, scouring the thick marble, building up a sweat; stretching to reach the corners of the huge mirror, the silver beading around the glass where the scum settled. When I finished cleaning all the rooms I'd take off my trainers and sink my bare feet into the pale wool carpet. I'd walk quietly through the house, along the hallways breathing it in. It felt like I was drinking something in; taking it in over my skin, as if I became the carpet and the walls and the air in the rooms and there was no separation between us. I'd take off my clothes, like an animal in a forest, shedding everything. I'd peel off my t-shirt and my skirt, leave them in a pile in the master bedroom. Walking naked, staring in the reflections of the paintings, seeing myself moving through the rooms. I'd glide past the painting in the hallway leading to the guest bathroom — a red-eyed hawk, its talons wrapped around the body of a small bird. I'd run my hands along the walls, trace my fingers around the flowery velvet motifs. I'd lie on their bed and stare at the ceiling. The ceiling fan unmoving, the lights piped through the roof, spotlighting the room. I'd cross the room and sit at the dressing table staring at the woman in the mirror. A strange, bony woman. The severe line of fringe across her forehead. Her face, still, like a mask, her eyes a thousand miles away. She was always shivering, I could see goosebumps on her bare arms. She'd sit there watching me. Sometimes her mouth would open, sometimes she'd answer the voices in her head, sometimes I'd see her lips moving. I'd watch her cry sometimes. Watch her remember things. Sometimes she laughed. I'd watch her dress, pulling her t-shirt over her head, straightening her skirt, getting back into her clothes.

Driving home I'd stop at the lay-by before the motorway on-ramp. Smoke a cigarette, then turn the car around, getting further and further away before I turned back. I'd find myself there again, sitting waiting in the lay-by, cars whizzing past. Preparing for the feeling when I opened my front door. I'd try to avoid the kitchen, try not to look at the telephone on the bench. Isolated, swimming in a moat of darkness.

One afternoon I heard a car pull up in the driveway, the crunch of shoes over the paving stones, the key in the lock, the front door opening. I was standing in the kitchen watching a car make its way down to the boat ramp, a red canoe shuddering on its roof rack. Staring out at the rain beating at the windows.
A voice called out.
"It's me Delia."
I'd almost forgotten she was real.
I heard her walk down the hallway, open the door to their bedroom. I heard the wardrobe open. She walked into the kitchen with a towel wrapped around her head. Her skirt soaked tight to her skin, shrunk in a lopsided ripple around her knees. Dripping dark spots over the slate tiles as she moved. I recognised the skirt, heavy textured, navy crepe, hanging in her wardrobe.
"I'm sopping wet," she laughed. I smelled wine on her breath. "I've been lunching." She rolled her eyes. "One of those days . . . God knows I've needed it lately." She slipped off her heels, dropped them with a clunk on the tiles. Water trickled along the pale lines of grout. She opened the cupboard above the fridge, reached for a glass, poured water from the purifier, it spilled over the bench.
"You know Delia, I really appreciate what you do for us. That feeling when you arrive home and everything is fresh." She breathed in deeply, swung around the kitchen. "It turns a new page, allows you to feel brighter." She laughed. "God, I suppose it's just dirt to you."
I smiled, glanced out of the window. The car had made its way to the edge of the boat ramp. A man got out, set the red canoe in the water gently. He climbed in. The glint of his metallic helmet. His boat, a speck starting out. His oars pushing through the waves with sure, rhythmical strokes. I thought about Malcolm's helmet on the rack in the garage, hanging beside mine on a hook above the gardening tools. Hedge clippers, secateurs, everything lined

up in rows. I remembered the apple tree we'd planted last year in the back garden, its slim, twiglike branches, the fuzzy sweetness of its buds, how it would need pruning. I started to think about driving home.

I sometimes wonder what she thought happened to me when I didn't go back. That envelope resting against the same blue glass ornament waiting for me. Arriving home and finding everything dirty, just how they'd left it. The breakfast dishes on the counter, the teaspoons crusted with egg. A sticky film over everything. And I wondered if she left the envelope the week after when she couldn't get hold of me? When she found out the phone number I gave her was fake. I imagined accidentally bumping into her somewhere, shopping, or driving past in her car, and I thought if that happened I'd pretend we'd never met.
I didn't try to find another house, but I often think about being there for those few hours in all that richness. The ozone from the sea, the taste of salt on the wind. Looking out over the view, the mist slowly disappearing. I remember the layout of all those rooms, the paintings I passed to get to the kitchen, the bathrooms, the master bedroom. I close my eyes sometimes, lean up close to the wallpaper, press my cheek and feel the velvet. I remember it so vividly, more vividly than any house.

Rapunzel
Alisha Brown

Snatched, they say. As though the stars
had not shown her my face in the sky
and said: here. This one. We have made
her for you […] And so the story goes.
The baby taken, the sun cast into eternal
shadow, the womb of the world rent
open by interminable grief, et cetera,
et cetera […] Jealous fools. I was old
enough to know the texture of brambles
between my thighs, thorns to pierce
a prince's prying eyes or soften into
morning dew beneath her tongue […]
Funny how every girl is a child until
a man or a moon decides otherwise
[…] And they will always make witches
of women who dare to read the hidden
language of things, who seek the swirling
tidepools and bathe, breasts free and
floating […] They will always make
a victim of the one who leaves her mother
for another lady in the dead of night […]
I hear it makes their own grief less ravenous.
Covers their animal in thicker cloak
[…] For that is what we are, after all;
just myth and membrane and the memory
of something more savage. Something
less ashamed to cast a shadow […] Mine
makes me breakfast and kisses me back
with an open mouth […] She is a terrifying
thing […] Braiding my hair with those
long fingers, saying she wants more of me,
more of me, dares me to grow until
I cannot be contained […] Don't you see?

It had to be a tower. How else could
we love but a hundred feet above it all [...]
Not hidden, but hiding. Not captive,
but captivated each and every cherry
sunset by the paling light over her lips,
her eyes [...] Where else could we
lock our hips and rock the world asleep
but here, the nightbirds, each day
our fable etched a millimetre deeper
into each other's tingling skin [...]

I fed my femininity to an ocean bird
Alisha Brown

I don't know what it means to be a woman.
From where I stand in these rockpools,
seawater nuzzling my ankles
with cool salt-crystal licks, it seems to me
that I am as much current as body,
let alone a woman's body –

that soft but too-soft never-quite-soft-enough
touched, touching, untouchable
don't touch me please touch me, please
that snakebite seductress hairflick
that kiss you goodnight, sweet child
that calloused hand on the saucepan lid
that same hand between my thighs, yours,
squeezing, earthworn and warm.

I don't know what it means to be anything
other than constant cell-flicker
eyes crinkling upward
my skin seeking light, seeking shade
this belly wanting soup or song
or the oceansigh of an ultrasound
pressed to the rising tide of a new baby's heart.

A white-faced heron stands
beside me in the shallows, patient.
I nudge a wriggling fish towards her beak.
Above, our same sun will soon appear
in its usual place, stroking the thin line
of the horizon over and over until it bursts.

Love Language
Clare Testoni

Have you eaten? Here I have some biscotti, not my best, too much sugar on the top. *Mangare*! Eat! You are too skinny and I worry that mother of yours – she does her best, I know – but a girl like you needs to eat well, it is how we are made in this family.

What's that? Are you recording? Where is the microphone? It is so small. Okay, okay, *allora*, I tell you then.

I was twenty-three in 1955 and a man from the village came to my parents and told them that his son was in Australia and needed a wife. There was no work and no money, none! I might like to have gone to university like you, or to typing school but there was no money. So my parents ask me, of course they ask me, and there were no young men in my village and I remember him, your Nonno, from when I was younger and my family knew his family. So, I marry him. But he was in Sydney already and I couldn't travel without getting married first. So I wore my wedding dress and my brother he stand where the groom would stand and I say the vows to the priest and sign the paper but I don't get married to your Nonno in person.

Lots of women did this then, it was what you did if you want to find a husband and you were not rich or too pretty. I was very shy, *timida*, and I was not good at talking to boys. I spend all my time in the garden with my Nonna helping grow things. I was a good girl but sometimes being a good girl does not get you what you want, eh? Like those loose clothes you wear, why are you hiding *bambolina*? You are not helping yourself. You are so beautiful but the boys will not know if you wear such potato sacks.

So, I have to pack to come to Australia and I pack the lace and the sheets my Nonna made for me. Things for a new home, like I have here in that chest for you one day. I pack my clothes, but back then we not have so many things. Not this five pairs of blue jeans and buy a new dress every day that they do now. No, I only have a few dresses.

I pack a book on how to learn English that my parents buy me, and a photograph of your Nonno. And before I go my Nonna, she was a brave woman you know, five of her children died but she was so strong and kind, Nonna give me seeds from the plants in her garden. This is a very special thing for her, these little bags of seeds that she keeps, *senti*, it is the secret to Italian cooking. The whole world loves the pizza and the pasta now, but back then no *Australiani* I meet had eaten a real tomato.

I am very lonely when I live here. You Nonno, he does not talk much. He is a very well dressed man, tall – not many tall men in my village. He looked like Marcello Mastroianni, more handsome than he had when he was a boy. The Australian girls love him. But he is very shy, too. Very, very quiet. He does not look at me in the eyes but down at his hands which he is always doing this... what you call this?
Tiddlie thumbs?
Twiddle?
Da vero? molto strano.
Anyway, he play with his hands all the time when he took me home. We did not know how to speak to each other and he work all the time. He built houses like lots of *Italiani* and left early in the morning, before the sun is up. After work he would go to the club with the other boys.

I was alone all the time. Australia was not like the village where everyone talks to each other, where people go together to the market or take the laundry down the street. I had my own washing machine! *Molto moderno!* I felt I was a very rich lady. But, no one to talk to. At church, they are all Irish and no one says hello. I try talking to my neighbour who was an old lady but she is not patient with my bad English. I hear her calling us "those dirty wogs" to her husband. I ask your Nonno what this means and he tells me not to talk to the neighbours.

So, no friends, no English. I am always in the garden. You see it now and you think it has always been this way, but at first it was very bad soil, very bad. So I dig and I make the soil rich like it was in the mountain soil back home and I plant the seeds from my Nonna. I plant *pomodoro, e melanzana, e zucca* for eating. I plant *basile e origano* for flavour. And I plant *salvia e ginepro* for good fortunes.

I watch them grow and I not miss my mother so much, not miss my Nonna. I think also, 'if I can cook beautiful Italian food for my husband, he will talk to me'. My mama always say that food is love. It's true! So I wait and I grow my garden and I hope my husband will like it.

Is it still recording, *caro*?
Where is the red light?
Do you want some coffee? Just pause him and I will make you some.

Allora, so, the fruit trees grow and the vegetables get fat and red and my skin is brown from being always in the garden. It is like I am back in Italy in my garden. Sometimes I think my Nonna is there with me. I pick the tomatoes and the eggplants and I make *pasta al forno* just the way we have back home. I am a good cook, you know this, and these were like no verdure, vegetables, the *Australiani* have ever eaten. This was a very good meal I make him. I put on a nice dress and I dress the table with all the lace from my wedding box. You know *caro*, in Italian the word for table *il tavolo* is male but the word for a table that is dressed for eating is female, *la tavola*. It says a lot about Italian peoples, no?

13

He comes home and he sits at my table and he eats my food. But, he says nothing. Nothing. He eats and then he turns on the radio and we sit in total silence! He doesn't even eat much food. I have a whole dish of the best pasta you have ever eaten and he does not even clean his plate. This man I don't know, who doesn't want to know me, is the only man I can talk to, that speaks my language, and he doesn't want to talk to me.

After that, I get very sad. I stop cleaning the house or dressing nice. I have no babies on the way, no friends, so I am always in my garden. He notice this then. He notice that I am ugly and sad now. He asks me why I am not dressing nice no more, why are there runs in my stockings and no curls in my hair, and I tell him, there is no point.

So, I get a knock on the door from the priest who comes into my house but I don't know what he says. He is smiling and I smile and he ask me questions in English, but I not know what he says. I point for him to sit – "*ti piacerebbe sederti*?" He sits and I bring him some food. A plate of *arancini* I make, filled with the vegetables from my garden. He brings out his bible and we pray together. We both speak the Latin. But, when he takes a bite of my *arincino* there is a miracle.

"*Li delizioso!*" He cries, and he is very surprised. He is speaking Italian without knowing.
"*Che cosa sta succedendo?*" He asks while he is looking at the *arincino* in his hand.

I did not know what is happening either. But, he was speaking Italian perfectly. I want to cry I am so happy. I tell him in Italian how lonely I am, not speaking the language, and he understands me. He nods, he cries. We pray and thank god for the miracle that let us speak to each other. We talk for many hours until the *arancini* are all gone and his Italian become English again and he does not know what I am saying.

14

That night I try to tell my husband what happened. I tell him that the priest came but he just nods and eats and goes out for a beer with his friends. I have asked him to have his friends over, that I will cook and that they can play cards and smoke, I don't care. But, he likes to go out. He put on his jacket and he reach for me with his hands, as if he is going to touch my face. But no, he put them in the pockets, he look at the floor and leave.

The next day the priest is back with some women from the church. I am dressed better this day and the house is clean again. I serve them *antipasti* with the tomatoes from my garden sliced very thin and salted well, a sprinkle of basil. That is all you need when they taste very good. The women had very fine hats on, very nice shoes. I was glad I had worn my best dress. They smiled and were very friendly. They raised their eyebrows at eating only tomato, but one bite and they understand. After the first bite they can open their mouths and they speak Italian like elegant ladies from *Roma*.

They laugh and they marvel as we talk about art and religion and fashion. They understand I am not stupid or some "dirty wog" now that we can speak the same. Now they know I am clever and cultured and they see that Italy is a land of culture. I tell them that I have seen The Sistine Chapel by Michelangelo Buonarroti and they are very impressed that I have been to the holy heart of the church. They drink my good Italian coffee and the priest discusses what this miracle must mean. That they must make me and the Italians of the church welcome. When they leave, I am so happy. I go and I begin making *sugo* from all my tomatoes to keep this miracle safe.

Again, I try and tell my husband about my day but again he does not look at me, does not speak. I tell him that the church is going to have a *festa del la pasta* to welcome us and the other Italians. That everyone will bring Italian food. His hands play with each other while he listens to me, he looks as the floor but he seems happy. I can tell because he flicks his eyes up to mine and he does a very small, *piccolino*, smile. I am so happy I throw my arms around him. But he steps back, it is too much. He tells me that he cannot go to *la festa*. He is busy. He sleeps on the sofa that night, not even in our bed.

He was very quiet your Nonno. Always. He did not know how to say what was inside him. It took me a long time to read him, to translate what he did not say. It was easier once I had your father and his brothers. He could talk to them, he loved children, children were easy, especially boys. He never learn to talk to women, except me.

Allora, so the big festa was given and I give my *sugo* to all the women in the church and told them how to make pasta. They came into my kitchen and ate my biscotti and we shared jokes that make much more sense in Italian than in English. They invited some other Italians who I did not know, men and woman from another church. The priest was so excited, he invites the bishop and the whole church is hung in *tri-colori*, red, white, green. I make many, many dishes, my garden is almost bare. I pluck the basil down to his stick, and it is the end of summer so I use all the tomatoes. I make lemon biscotti from my lemons and a cake with my strawberries.

Oh *mio caro*, when I get there people are already eating and talking in *Italiano*. I was crying. It was like being home in my village to see everyone, children and women and men all laughing and singing in my language. After a year of no speaking to anyone now the words flow like wine. Everyone enjoys *il miracolo. Gli Australiani* and *gli Italiani* mix and dance, and the children play. The *Australiani* sing Italian songs they did not know but when you speak Italian you are Italian. They play *bocce* and soccer. The women are better dressed than ever and the men wear sharp suits in Italian style with broad shoulders. My husband does not come, but everyone asks for him. Everyone asks me about him, people ask me about everything. They are interested in me now, like I am clever and beautiful. It was a wonderful night.

Of course, after, there was no food left in my garden. So when the peoples visit now we not understand each other again. We smile and nod and they help me with my English. It is better than before. Now they know me, they remember what I was like in my own language.

The next vegetables and fruit I grow did not have *il miracolo* inside them. Maybe the seeds have been too long in the ground of Australia. Maybe god only let it be once to open up my neighbours. People still eat my food, it is still delicious even if it is not magic. My English got better and I meet other Italians who came to the festa. So, I not so lonely anymore.

Your Nonno and I still only spoke a little. But, now I was not so shy, *non così timida*. One night when he came home I had no food for him. I had not cooked anything. Instead, I walk to him and I put my hands on his face, like this, slowly. I put my arms around him, *piano piano*. I not say anything. I just touch him. I understand when he touch me back, it was *mio miracolo*, we spoke the same language then. Your father was born later that year, and things were better then.

Basta! Stop the recorder now. I am done. I am an old lady who cannot talk so much. Before you go I want you to take some *marmellata* for your mother, okay?

Bewitched & Between
Beth Spencer

Six o'clock is the witching hour. Samantha
flying in side-saddle on a broomstick,
burning the dinner, transforming into a black
cat, leaping into What's-His-Name's arms.

I lie on the green carpet, transfixed by the tv
pretending I can't hear my mother
as she calls and calls from the kitchen.
'Girls! Come set the table for dinner.'

Who could believe that Sam, able to conjure
anything with a twitch of her nose, would
willingly trade wizardry for a kitchen whizz?
Now that's a fantasy.

Ever-loyal helpmeet to Derwood as he
manipulates desire and peddles illusion,
casting his dreary capitalist spells.
But who's the real creative genius?

All those contortions and tricks
so necessary to enable the man
of the house to believe he's the head.
The laugh track — hahahahaha!

And who can miss the way Sam keeps
coming down with mysterious ailments.
Such as, finding all the doors and windows
sealed against her. (Trapped in the house!)

Or the time everything she touches
turns to gold. (A gilt complex!) And the day
every sneeze creates a bicycle or tricycle.

'Totally logical,' announces Doctor Bombay.

'In fact, it's cycle-logical!' He twirls his glorious
moustache, ponders, and diagnoses the problem.
She has been suppressing her powers.
The solution? Start using them!

Curled on the Fler lounge, I notice how Sam
flinches at Darrin's anger, his constant criticism
if things go a tiny bit wrong (Julius Caesar in the
kitchen, for instance, instead of a caesar salad).

That hint of violence under the laugh track.
But what do you expect if you agree
to give up your powers? All the other witches
see Sam as a fallen woman, a drudge to a man.

Meanwhile, look! Here's Serena —super fun
gerroovay 'Dark Lady' to Sam's 'Fair Maiden'.
'Fly me to the moon,' croons one of her lovers
and next minute there he is, up among the stars.

Another is turned into a bedwarmer when she
tires of him. Everything so literal and full of puns.
Like dreams. With Endora perched on the stairs,
the mother-in-law of all jokes come home to roost.

For half an hour each weeknight I am part of a coven.
Revelling in a Wiccan heritage. This quicksilver world
where the galaxy is one's backyard. And while men
can be a part of it, women rule supreme.

The queer, the magical, the feminine
— the irruption of the repressed —
opening all the doors and all the windows.
Letting in the stars.

Diary of a Maid, Asia Minor
The story of Judith from the Apocrypha
Jude Aquilina

Today the sun was kind, yesterday's cloud severed by its
radiance. Again, I sewed for Judith widow of Bethulia, working
my threads from the first blush of dawn to crepuscular vespers.
The bodice is finished and hangs on a hook behind the door, the
neckline dives deeper than any I have sewn before. As I fitted the
lining of her skirt, a blackbird sang from a high bough and I
blessed each stitch on these cumquat layers where already a
sheath is concealed like a snake in autumn leaves. . . Tonight I
heard the widow speaking to the spirits: 'Dear husband, give me
strength,' she pleads. And when she visits me, she removes her
widow's weeds, tries on the dress, parades before me with a face
by turns humble, brave and terrified.

Tomorrow I will line the palm-rope basket strong enough to hold
bread, wine, roasted grain, a cornucopia of roots and fruits, all we
have. I'm certain the basket will carry her quarry. . . I saw him
once through a spyhole in the wall which both protects and pens
us in like animals for the slaughter. He smiled. I fled. I will pad
the basket with powdered orris root to absorb any blood that may
spill.

A New Moon last night blessed our return. At sunrise, the
Assyrian army fled when they found Holofernes, felled like a
giant palm tree, a necklace of red around his headless trunk. And
after we rested, Judith told me that his face changed from lust to
astonishment as it rolled.

The Sabbath. After thirty-four days, a stream of dusty people
poured through the gates to celebrate freedom gained, fields
reclaimed. They drank like beasts from the springs. Deep into
the green well Judith threw the fiery dress, our work put to rest in
quiet water. And Holofernes' skull lies inside my woven nest in a

rocky crevice ninety-two cubits west of Bethulia. Tomorrow I will begin a night-gown of gossamer blue for our saviour Judith, of Judah, so she may rise to the stars and sleep soundly again on the feathery down of the milky way.

Note: Dairy of a Maid, Asia Minor was previously published in *On a moon spiced night*, Wakefield Press, South Australia

Caroline Herschel
Alicia Sometimes

'she whom the moon ruled' - Adrienne Rich

the ebb of calculations & deductions. all night star seducing
exhausting tea making & sidereal astronomy
collapsing horse manure
into glue to hold
the heavens straight
a soprano waiting for the nod
to gather life's dust for hobby. to sweep some nebulae her way

she rules in notebooks for precision. wants to find a Lady's comet
& notices changing clusters & twin lights circling each other
nestling swans. she is the galaxy. she is a magnet.
she is
home. William has just discovered Uranus
her pride expands to the swelling moments
of the Big Bang. her eyes
dizzy at times while her fingers crack pencils
she feels her brother did all the

(I am a mere tool…I know how dangerous it is for women
to draw too much notice…)

sharpening

after William, she catalogues another 2500 positions
Nothing—not sleep or meals take her away
from this proven love. for 97 years
she emits curiosity
for all years after, she delivers
a slice of the unknown

Carolyn Beatrice Parker
Alicia Sometimes

It is a silvery metal
in a dark room
blue-skewed glow
excited by decay

Does Parker
hold the polonium in her hands
does she ever breathe it in?

working government top-secret
with this radioactive element

—The Dayton Project—
research and development
during World War II
part of the Manhattan Project
building the first atomic bombs

first Black woman in the U.S.
to have a postgraduate degree
in physics
two masters—the other in mathematics

dedicated, hardworking, afire

little is known of her work
within the team constructing secrets:
polonium-based neutron
initiators kindling pressure

Dayton Project employees
not allowed to eat in processing areas
scrubbing down before they leave

(some have contaminated bobby pins)

assistant professor
in physics at Fisk University
close to completing a doctorate at MIT

so much more to discover
from this sharp ascending scientist
her time far too short

atomic number 84

leukaemia age 48

Persephone
Brittany Riley

[puh · seh · fuh
· nee]
Read first *war*
or *peace*
depending on
your truest
desires.

Death brings *war*   Death brings *peace*

Cross your
threshold
go forth

Humble
servants   Beauty

of Hades must   is infinite matter

right the   bound to ecstasy
malpractices   Benevolence is
of humanity   rewarded

Lady Justice   finally
with an assortment   after
of thistles   all
and a blood moon   this time
in each scale   disrobe
as gifts for you   unapologetically

especially   and gaze at your
                                                      collection

for you,

Precious

Bitter grapefruit.
Straight from the
rind.

Human
sentiments are not
wasted
on this plane
Mortal screeches
are cabaret
for the revellers

Dread is
a broken-down
carousel
left to rust
Unwanted,
forlorn

Heed the sign:
BROKEN HEARTS
ONLY

Shades of snakeskin
cool to the touch
do not ogle
at Medusa

of contemporary
realism,

Precious

Flower nectar.
Straight from the
chalice.

Gallery 1.
dandelion
sprinkles
harp bows
lamb bleats
coconut cream
soliloquy poetry
~
Gallery 2.
pearl strings
kitten purrs
vanilla pods
fairy meadows
wine waterfalls

All love
is requited
now as

evil doesn't
blossom
in purity,
it
wilts

Baseball caps
don't mask your
identity,
Phantom

Pluck stars

for sparkling

bouquets

pay for your
wickedness

and plunge into
tide pools of
jewels
in sheer pastel
dresses
and blush
lipstick

Tear your chest

open

to reveal your runes

and bleed

gather ocean
ornaments as
keepsakes

Fear breeds fear
doesn't that feel
better now
it was all in your
head

respire easily

underwater

to morph

with Utopia
below

see?

Consent to darkness

it was (in) you all
along,
Precious

Paradise does
not have
an expiration
date,
Precious

Soar like a crow.
You're free.

Soar like a dove.
You're free.

Crown of
bones.

Crown of
seashells.

You wear it well.

Thinking about the immortality of the crab
Arielle Bodenstein

'Were we led all that way for Birth or Death?' - T. S. Eliot

Waking up to the smell of ammonia makes you wonder if you've died. A horrible, sterile death. The kind of death where Margret is at the end of the bed, hands clasped like a grieving Saint Peter, saying some rubbish like 'well, she's finally found peace' as she lets two perfect tears fall down her cheek. Of course, Margret would have perfect tears. Hamish would be behind her, talking to the doctors like he wasn't just a forklift operator with a gambling problem. He'd tell them they bungled the procedure, that this whole bloody place is dog's breakfast and that he knows a guy who'd bring down the entire operation you best believe it. Later, he'd pocket a twenty from Simon in the carpark, with the kind of smile that says I told ya she wouldn't make it. And then there was mum. Poor, hopeless mum—rolling cigarettes in her lap as if nothing in the world was amiss. If it weren't for her posture, she might have looked regal perched amongst the carnations like that. But mum was never regal. She was the creased cloth of a still life; a pale backdrop for ripe fruit.

With the ammonia came memories of Dad. Each night after work he would sit in their yellow fibreglass tub till the water went cold and emerge shivering in a sweet cloud of bergamot and jasmine. Still the smell remained. It was as though he'd been steeped in alkaline; a solution of chlorine and bleach that stained more than the hems of his work pants. One morning mum found him, blue-lipped in the bath. A foetus had fallen out of a cow he was tasked with gutting. Unsure of what to do, the men had thrown it in a bin of flayed heads. The abattoir was windowless, but the eyes of a hundred mothers watched them do it. Some things aren't so easily washed off.

The hospital room had smelled of dad that morning. Dad's ammonia skin and the floral scent of soap. There was rubber too; plastic tubing and powdered latex gloves, the sharp peppermint on Simon's breath as he leant in close, the laundry powder on his collar and the faint tobacco on mum's lap.

But the baby didn't smell like anything to me.

'Do you have those spots you just can't seem to get rid of? How about stains that never seem to come out? What you need is Invincible by Clorox: the only cleaner strong enough to get out those invincible spots. With our new, secret formula, Invincible's scrub-tastic power will have your stains out faster than your husband can make them!'

I didn't expect to find God on the infomercial channel. But there He was – a man in a blue polo, slashing prices on my salvation. He was the true authority on purity and the women in the videos followed His every command. They sprayed, soaked and scoured. It was as though He could solve their messy, failed lives in an instant. Once downcast and dejected, they now beamed before an audience of glistening tiles and starched fabrics in every shade of white. They didn't seem to notice that their houses smelled like hospital rooms and death. They had been saved by the blue polo God with frosted tips.

For today only, He offered redemption at an unbeatable price. He'd even throw in free delivery if you called this number now. It seemed like a fair trade for tight curls and pearl earrings and a dress with perfect pleats. I could sashay through a kitchen in kitten-heels, with desires so modest they'd be met with geometric splash-backs and innovative tupperware designs. Simon would come home to the smell of pot-roast and brandied apples. I'd greet him at the door with the baby on my hip. It wouldn't be crying. It would have flushed cheeks and a face like sunshine.

'Well God be gracious, now I'm seeing things. You haven't made a meal since Shirley Pollykoff sold coats!'

Canned laughter fills the sitting room.

'Why, it's Invincible darling. Its new formula removes stains up to three times faster than your average household cleaning product. I even had time to make a pie.' My efforts are rewarded with an artificial ovation.

'Well, just hold on a hot minute now, sweetheart. What about those real tough stains?'

'Invincible does it all darling!'

'Even the bathroom?'

'Why it's true! Just see for yourself.'

Simon twirls me around and we appear, as if by magic, on a new set. But the bathroom doesn't look like the ones from the infomercials. In fact, it hasn't been cleaned at all. A pile of clothes lie by the door and little shards of facial hair fill the sink. A dark spot of mould has formed on the ceiling above the tub. The air is laden with ammonia and bleach. Simon doesn't seem to notice. He stands with his hands on his hips and whistles.

'Well, I say. Talk about out damned spot!' He flashes a charming grin to an invisible camera and waits for the laugh-track.

It never comes. The only sound is from the tap, which drips into the stagnant bath water and sends ripples over dad's blue-lipped body.

Finally, the baby starts to cry.

'So apparently everyone's marriage goes through a kind of midlife crisis where you end up hating the very person you swore to be with forever. At least that's what a long-time couples counsellor is claiming in their new book. What do we reckon ladies? Do you hate your husbands?'
'Well James and I just welcomed a little baby girl. I know! Thank you! So actually I'd say that we've never been happier than we are now.'

Liar.

'Well, you're in the second phase, right? The book says you fall in love first and everything's peaches. Next, you become partners and really start to build your lives together. Until you

hit the fifteen year mark and in comes the Disillusionment
Phase.'
'You know this really shocked me when I read it. I think it's way
off. I was disillusioned after about five!'

I could still see Simon standing before me in the grocery
store checkout line where we'd met. I'd never witnessed someone
unpack their trolley in such an organised and considerate fashion.
There was something so endearing about the way he grouped his
dairy products together, like the chaos of life was manageable as
long as you kept your butter with your cheese. I hated shopping
centres, but in that moment, I had quietly hoped that the things in
his trolly never stopped coming; that we could exist in an eternal
loop of onions and aftershave. He kept apologising to the woman
behind the register for having so much stuff, even though he was
simply buying groceries and she was simply doing her job. Then
he apologised to me for making we wait.

It was impossible to be disillusioned with Simon. He was
exactly as he seemed. Still, there were things about him that were
infuriating. Like the way he dropped food on his lap whenever he
ate and the way he cleaned the crumbs up one-by-one with his
index finger once he noticed. There was the condescending
eyebrow raise he gave when he flossed and the gentleness with
which he folded his shirts. Or the fact that he insisted on eating
ice-cream with a fork. What was this phase called?

It had been worse since the baby. His instinct for
fatherhood was a relentless attack. Nothing felt more unnatural
than to speak with it, but for Simon it seemed so easy. He made
small talk about his day, the state of the world, or the true
meaning behind a nursery-rhyme. He philosophised with it over
pureed peas. And where does your mother stand on the great
carrot-pea debate? The whole exercise seemed pointless to me.

It was an offensively beautiful day outside when I tried to
tell him how I feel. Spring had been one horrible joke. I wanted to
rip out the flowers in our front-yard and tell the birds to be quiet.
Simon just watched me. I hated the way he did that too. Like he

was some kind of specialist, waiting for me to make a movement worthy of his observation—a soft sigh to add to his field notes. I refused to give him anything and after a while he said, 'I think you've just got the blues.'

And I said, 'that's not fair.'

'Well, what then? You tell me.'

'No. That's not fair. To blue.'

'What?'

'The blues. Why does everyone say that? Blue is such a nice colour.'

And he said, 'you know, sometimes I think you don't want anyone's help.'

I wonder if I should buy the book. A quick search tells me it's by a Jan Diamond—surely a pseudonym? Apparently not. Jan lives in New York and specialises in manopause. According to Jan, men are a bag of dicks. Not exactly a groundbreaking study. I could buy it just to spite Simon—leave it open on the bedside table. See, I do want help and actually you'll find that you're the real problem here and I'm entirely perfect. But frankly, I didn't trust Jan. Her bio says she's been divorced five times, which apparently makes her an expert on the matter and not just a terrible couples counsellor. Jan must feel disillusioned a lot.

'Three people, including a four year old boy's mother, have been injured in a serious crash on the Motorway going North.'

The news was always a reminder that I didn't belong to myself anymore. That I was a mother now, and that when I died I'd be nothing but a dead mother. I could kill myself in the most selfish way imaginable—gut myself with kitchen knife and write my name in blood all over the windowless walls and some tidy reporter with perfect cleavage would still say with rehearsed sincerity that a new-born baby's mother had unfortunately taken her own life last night, but the child, thankfully, was reported safe.

'Now you're gonna want to start off with two sticks of a butter and about half a cup of sugar and let that mix real nicely for a few minutes. I just think these are the perfect little after school treats. I know my kids sure love them and I'm sure yours will too!'

Imagine coming home to lemon bars. Sticky citrus fingers and golden curd. Little crumbs of shortbread on the floor. The only thing mum ever produced in our kitchen was boiled chickens because dad wouldn't eat anything else. Chickens, dad said, are just unworthy birds. There's a reason we call cows beef and pigs pork. Chicken is just chicken. And chicken shit is just chicken shit. And those are the only two facts of life, you hear?

Margaret and I would sit in front of the TV for hours, plates of cold chicken breast and tomato sauce on our laps. Margaret always got to pick the channels. We'd watch Skippy, The Price is Right, and the evening weather report. I'd fall asleep in front of The Penthouse Club, only to wake up and realise Hey Hey It's Saturday! Most of the time it was The Brady Bunch. I loved Carol's perfect golden hair and the way she appeared—at the exact moment of need— in a kitsch collared dress, or a two-piece suit in avocado green. Carol was almost mythical.

'Marcia, Marcia, Marcia! It's all I hear about. Everything comes so easy to her.'

'Oh, Jan! Some of us are good at one thing, and some of us are good at the other. Get out and about on the town and find what you're good at!'

After the episode I asked mum what I was good at and she said I was damn good at ruining her day. Eventually, I stopped asking her anything at all. It was as though she became less and less interested in life the more she lived it. First, she lost interest in boiling chickens. Chickens, mum said, are just the weird cousins at the bird family dinner. You don't want to talk to them, but they probably need love more than anyone and if your father says otherwise it's because he's a bigot and a racist. Then, she lost interest in showering, in leaving the house, in talking. Finally, she lost interest in us.

The whole time Margaret acted like nothing was wrong. She'd prop herself up on our ugly tartan sofa and attempt to detangle mum's hair with her favourite pink comb, strands of silver falling in her lap like soft filaments of silk. She'd hum along to the theme song while she worked and laughed whenever Peter said pork chops and apple sauce ain't that swell. Mum didn't seem to notice anything was playing on the screen, or that she was even in the room with us watching TV. She just sat there rolling cigarettes in her lap. She hadn't lost interest in that.

Margaret told everyone at school that we lived in a big mansion and that you had to pinky swear not to tell anyone but the real reason no one was allowed to come over was because mum was an undercover spy and our house was full of deadly criminals that she was keeping a real close eye on.

We'd been watching a lot of Matlock Police that week.

When mum disappeared for a few days it was because she was trapped inside a genie's bottle somewhere in the Pacific. The great adventures of mum followed whatever Margaret and I were watching at the time. One moment she was meeting the prime-minister. The next, she was solving mysteries in a barely functioning jalopy with a gorilla named Tracy. She was a witch, a rockstar, she was in New York being 'That Girl.'

But she was never mum.

Margaret still lived in this made-up world where mum was Carol Brady and everything was groovy and neato! It was worse after she met Hamish. They were in whatever hell-scape came after the Disillusionment Phase. But you'd never know it. Marg was always perfect composure this and help yourself to a shortbread that and gee isn't every day a blessing from the Lord?

It was probably why mum preferred Margaret; the daughter that didn't make her take anti-depressants because all they're good for is reminding you that you're depressed. The only time mum had shown me anything resembling love was after the baby was born. She called me and said hello and didn't ask how the mother was doing—terribly, if you'd care to know—and in a voice I didn't recognise said 'she's perfect, by the way.' I wanted nothing more than to exchange pleasantries over the landline, to be a daughter and say things like 'so nice of you to call' and 'please come and visit soon!' But all I could think about was how my whole life I'd tried to be perfect for her and now that I'd finally done something right, it wasn't me who got any of the credit.

> *'Just let that simmer away for a few minutes. What you don't want is for it to come up to a boil.'*

I wonder what lies the baby will tell about me? If it will say that the horrible indifference felt by its mother was the result of some kind of freak accident, or an experiment gone wrong. That it wasn't just the boredom of another empty hour spent traipsing through the living room, back and forth across the carpet—who would tire first?

> *'What do you want to say about yourself today? That you're a superstar? That you're out to play? That you're a woman on the move? Whatever you want to say, say it in Blooming Colours: the new shades by Maybelline.'*

I wanted to say that there was an overwhelming vacancy within me. That it wasn't the blues or the mean reds or any of the blooming colours. That it was a murky, muted grey.

> *'Give a woman's touch, a woman's care, and a woman's compassion to your goodbye with White Lady Funerals: a woman's understanding.'*

And that when I finally woke up to the smell of ammonia and carnations, it didn't feel like the beginning of life at all. It felt like death, my death. And everyone was there to celebrate it, pink helium balloons and all. Congratulations! It's over! You've done it! And when mum rolled her cigarettes and Margaret cried her perfect little tears and Simon placed you in my arms, I didn't feel anything for you— for this perfect, fragile thing I was bound to let down.

'Among the first full moon of winter, an army of crabs materialise. For the past year, they've been feeding in deeper waters. Now, they march across the seagrass plains. They're not seeking mates, nor are they laying eggs. They have simply come here for one thing—to grow.'

The TV was full of skeletons—clambering piles of calcium and bone. They scuttled across a screen of blue and buried their legs in the sand.

'Like all members of the decapod family, the body of the crab is enclosed in a hard exoskeleton. To survive, it must break out. But the decision to molt is not one easily made. Leaving the carapace means the crab will be entirely without protection. Now soft and delicate, it is entirely vulnerable to predators. Yet, choosing to stay within its casing will surely result in death, as the crab's body continues to outgrow its own home. They must therefore discard this hard exterior, if the soft animal beneath it is to live on.'

There was a birth, certainly. I had watched it happen. A soft creature emerged in a thin white casing. Delicate, newborn flesh. Weightless wonder.

But there was a death, too. A carcass, almost identical, left behind to rot.

Gorgon
Romy Tara Wenzel

They took my name, the thorn-hearted men.
Annealed and beat it, reddened it with
Spiteful tongues until my name was glass.
Wild animals fled from it.

Before, together. We were small, earthern things.
Ate squid and cockles for supper.
My name and I, by campfire,
Pulled fables from the shadows.

The men reforged her. A shiny, robust name to
Focus their hatred; hard enough to cut holes in,
Sink lines and hooks into,
Catch hedge-witches and biddies with.

I did not know her. No longer did she
Play with frogs in the water.
No longer did my name talk with me, about
The numinous, luminous universe.

I tried to follow her, for a while.
I mirrored her backwards. I obeyed her.
She shamed me, made me small.
I lost sight of the marble-eyed world.

I weevilled through the cracks,
The floorboards. Through the doubts and
The questions. I broke the back of my self
And crawled through it. Until I was many.

She met me on equal ground, on legend's
Threshold. Now I thrill the infinite
Wings open wide as books,

Speak devotions of stories.

The world aches with my fire
I have priestesses, I have
Hives of students to honey the earth
Creatures winged, pawed and fearless.

I have so many names now
I forget I was once
Only darkness.

Rusałka
Kathryn Simons

The water is like air on my skin. My long hair cuts my vision into ribbons. I watch it like I used to when I was a child. The days bleed into one another. The ache in my neck has faded yet I remain in the inbetween. For a long time, I listened to the fish and birds whisper their tales, frayed by time and kept together through their telling. To the fish I listened most intently. Although I had spent my life marking the soil with my feet, I now felt kinship to those of the river. The fish spoke of Upes Māte, she who commands the waters of river and streams alike. They nudged me, they promised she would guide me as a daughter of the river.

I called upon Upes Māte, I prayed to her as if to my old God. Tell me what to do, show me my place, I begged. Tell me how to move beyond the end of my own story. But I received nothing but strange whispers in return.

Now as I look to the sky above, I wonder if the whispers mean anything at all.

I can still leave the water. Pulling myself from its currents, I climb onto the land. It is hard and unforgiving on my soft feet. The air is dry to my lungs now, so used to the smoothness of the water. I sit on the bank, in a pool of clear summer light, twisting and untwisting my hair. It has grown unnaturally since I made the river my home. As I hum the tune I sing in the river, a plea to Upes Māte, I am reminded of the stories of a peasant girl whose beautiful voice attracts the king, at once freeing and trapping her.

Voices startle me from my thoughts. My instinct is to slip back into the safety of the river, but I hesitate. I hide from the villagers I once lived with, something warns me of the pain and fear I would cause. But I often wish I could reach out and touch them. Few venture this far up the river, only the curious, the idle or the foolish. The voices sound close but they do not appear to be moving towards me. Curiosity pulls me closer. The pitch of the girl's voice reminds me of my own. It jolts me, stirring my memories up like a pebble thrown into a pond.

"Andris, please, stop being funny." The girl laughs but it is unnatural, forced. My mind becomes muddy with fear and I feel water burning my throat as memories bleed into my vision. My hand goes up to my neck, to the faded line. I stumble as I feel myself ripped apart again and the forest betrays my presence.

"Who's there?" a male voice calls. My vision clears enough for me to see them, the man and girl, across the clearing. They both look at me in something like fear, astonishment. I know my appearance, my long hair and deathlike skin, is like something out of a story. I have wandered too far; the thought is sharp in my mind.

The girl takes advantage of my appearance to squirm away from the man's grasp. Her fear steels something in me. I hold the man's gaze, even as the fear leaks from it and it takes on another edge. I feel the girl disappear and only then do I dare turn, hurrying over uneven ground. A muffled shout comes delayed, but I do not look back. My feet touch the river. Its currents embrace me, and I know I am safe.

The girl has unsettled me. Her look, her fear, her voice. She has awakened something in me and now, even as I feel the safety of the water, I carry the memory of its cruelty in my throat. I wander the forest more frequently. The fish worry at me as I pull myself out of the water, they warn me, not understanding that I am not like them.

It feels like months since the girl, but it might have been days. Without sleep to mark the days, I cannot hold time down. I have continued to pray to Upes Māte, but perhaps she cannot hear me from wherever she rests, for all that answers me is the constant lapping whispers.

I settle on a blanket of freshly fallen leaves, still soft yet already touched by Lapu Māte's hand. The mother of the forest has begun her travels, slowly turning the leaves to announce the coming of Veļu laiks, the time of the spirits. My senses are dulled

41

above water. While the river used to soothe me, now I find the way the air muffles my memories until the sounds are merely a strange melody more of a comfort.

I think of those stories, told in the dark months, where the characters always had a purpose, a pattern to follow. My mother used to tell me life was a story; we all had our own beginnings and ends. Remembering my own end might be more bearable should it not feel so jagged and untidy. Yet now I think of the girl and, while I have spent the past days resenting the pain the sight of her has caused, I realise she also gives me a kind of strength. The river saved me, and I saved her in turn. The river seems to appreciate the thought, as the whispers sharpen, and I can almost make out words.

The leaves warn me, but I am too slow to react. When I turn, I see him standing there. I recognise him instantly. He looks bewildered.

"I have been looking for you," he says. I stand, wary of the look in his eye. My skin prickles, I feel as if I am seeing with double vision. My memory covers my eyes like the running water of the river distorts the rocks on its bed. He speaks but I don't hear him. He comes closer and I feel the shift in the air. He grabs at me. I pull away and my foot slips into the river. Its touch jolts me, whispering along my skin. In my fear, the whispers shape into words and tug at my mind like a forgotten story. Long hair, deathless, hunted and hunter. I finally understand. My anger comes swift, like a river after rain, and with it something strange, a power now acknowledged.

"Let me go," I say. The words are barely above a whisper, but I give him a chance to run, to leave. A chance I wish I had been given. He claws at me like a beast from a fairy story. Both my feet are in the river now. The whispers of Upes Māte are loud in my ear. I smile at him, and he loosens his grip. He does not notice the water swell around him. He pulls me towards him, and I pull him under the surface, my hair wrapping around his limbs. Finally, his face turns from desire to fear. I hold him until the river fills him. Upes Māte's words ring in my ears, whispering through the water.

Rusałka, the water whispers, *Rusałka*.

Rusałka was previously published in The Saltbush Review, Issue 1.

Pink gum
Sara C. Motta

pink gum, plush carpet
cold ice, zip lock bag,
hard like a nipple
touched right
pert like my clit

silent night, barely lit
after zip lock bag
head lice
vomit
walking a tight rope with life

Indigenous, Jewess
limbs stretched
across class, culture, family
lines
impaled like Christ

if it weren't for
Magdalene's redemption
wench becomes priestess
exiled
returns to life

these mother's duties
don't become her
rubbing insistently
scraper in hand
imagining the eyes of inspection

without right, without inheritance
without desire
for a heteronormative

half-life;
hands and knees, it is then

fish-net tights, magpie oven glove
Menorah, second night
la puma negra prowls
emptiness
Black (w)holes as whores

tonight, Xmas decorations
watering succulents
breathing kundalini fire
riding
the dragon of erotic flight

Salome, Sarah Bernhardt
abuelita Lucrecia, nana Antoinette
telling tales of lacklustre adventure
reminding me
to fuck right, and often, and with who

I damn like.
I said I'd write a poem
about that pink gum on the plush carpet
I guess it didn't come out right
all crooked and queer

mixed up, mestizaje
burlando at the straight lines
constraints
dis-ordering, disdainful
of the empty lies of disembodied divinity.

The Destruction of Salomé ~ Demise of a Temptress
Paris Rosemount

The beginning is never where the real story begins
How dreadfully unsatisfying
If Iokonaan's erotically severed head
Were simply presented to Salomé
On that delightful silver platter
No, no – that would not have sufficed at all
We hunger for the sinful desire, that burning lust

In our shroud of anonymity, we shamelessly ogle
The nubile vixen
As she strips her layered veils
One delicately
perfumed
wisp
at a time
Oh dance for us, Salomé!
We are the silent voyeurs to your wicked burlesque

The ending is never the real ending, either
Salomé is no longer luminescent as a gilded lily in moonlight
But radioactive like a ghoulish she-devil
Under the eerie glow of a blood moon

Herod commands the destruction of this vile creature
The original tale, being a couple of millennia old
Is scant on the details surrounding said destruction
Perhaps ye olde-time folk were a more prudish bunch
But you out there, you're a bloodthirsty mob, are you not?
Surely you would like to know
How the soldiers encircled young Salomé like wolves

Night after night they had endured the torment
Of glancing furtively through their helmets

At this bewitching child-woman
She would lick her ruby lips in delight
As her stepfather plied her hungry mouth
With grapes, figs and juicy, ripe peaches
The juice would drip from the corners of her lips
And her pink tongue would flicker out to catch every drop
Like the greedy little serpent she was
Oh Salomé, how you tantalise by your very existence!

Well, you could not blame the soldiers, could you
For acting in the way that they did
They had so cruelly been led on by this teenage temptress
It surely had to have been her fault for having so aroused them
It is one of the oldest stories in one of the oldest books
She had been asking for it

And so they lined up, one by one (or sometimes two or three at a
time)
She possessed more than one orifice, after all
To ravage the virgin princess in such violent ways
That would surely have sent them spiralling into the pits of Hell
To join her in the afterlife

Perhaps the ancient storytellers were right after all
To have omitted such details from the Book of Time
Perhaps some things are better left unsaid

Holding Patterns
crone – mother – maiden
Kyla St Jaye

This morning there's salt in my mouth. On the edge of sunrise, the sea beats tangled in bird calls echoing in the distance off the scrub and granite. I am washed with light and tight in South Coast shadows. There's a lot to do. Boxes to tape, keys to find, washing to hang because it needs to be hung. And I'm hung in stories no one ever forgets. Stretched and semi-transparent, they take up more space than I remember. Like damp bed sheets, or ghosts. I slide in the barely blank spaces before the day, before they're too solid and stick in my throat, while I can still breathe. The mountains falter then recover, staggered on the half-dark horizon. A cow calls from a roo chewed paddock then plane engines rush sky. Roaring and low they circle scanning for sharks, lost fisherman or more likely, they're waiting for space to land. I'm holding. For just a moment. Hold until there's no breath left. I could hold on hold off hold them hard and close. Hold your bluff. Hold those aces. Hold. It's a roundabout word that pauses, then circles. Round and around it goes. There are boundaries to hold or forts or tongues, hold it together or hold them apart. I'm holding still.

And still after all this time.

My favourite thing to hold is her hand.

I've fast hands, they're sleight and bitten, and to my surprise they can still juggle oranges. My daughter sits on the back steps, her mouth drops open she claps her hands, 'Again! Do it again!' My hands smell like citrus, my hands are full of smoke. I hold them out solid and dark against the bleached sky.

In my backyard there's a fence, a line of lattice that sags and divides my neighbour's house from mine. In the mornings the lattice makes squares of light and shade, like a chessboard across her lawn. In the afternoons, the sun shifts and the chessboard swings to mine.

When I juggle, sometimes and to my surprise, I can see my neighbour. Her shape is hidden in the chessboard shadow, then in a lattice gap she is sudden and clear. She looks small and very alone. She stops sometimes to wave at my daughter, other times to narrow her eyes at me. At the letterbox she stops to open bills and council notices. Her hands shake and she takes a quick look to the sky. Sometimes she looks frightened, and I just can't bear to look at her. So I look back to my backyard, where I sit sometimes or smoke or juggle.

Though my backyard isn't really mine. It belongs to her. She is my landlord – I am her tenant.

The word tenant comes from the Middle English *tenir* which translates directly as hold. I'm her tenant. I hold – on one hand, anyway. On the other hand, I'm holding, I'm her tenet. Pick up the e drop the n; my hands smell like citrus and smoke. Tenet and tenant are close words, near divisible by a line of lattice. Tenet means doctrine, a principle or dogma that's held by a group of people. I hold and am held by a tenet: whose worth is weighed and marked like fruit and measured all the time.

'Appalling!' her voice sliced through the lattice sour and sharp like unripe apples. 'Those people! They think the world owes them something! It's the little girl I feel for. Fancy not being able to provide. Well, I've bloody well had enough!' She marched behind the lattice, across the chessboard squares of shadow and light. There was a game being played I should've understood. Phone in one hand and an envelope in the other, she marched to the back door, gave three-hard-knocks, dropped the envelope on the step and marched on back. With the sun sitting behind her, her shadow cast the length of the backyard.

I sat on the back stairs holding an eviction notice handwritten on floral stationary, holding my breath.

Her writing shook and looped across the page, like the cards my Nanna used to write, signing off: With Love, Be Good. The South Coast wind kicked and unwound. I looked at the line drawn between her and I – a line more imposing and less precise than

49

the chessboard shadow of a lattice fence. Where I saw her age, she saw my poverty. More clearly, we both saw an absence of worth. That night while she slept, I counted my daughter's fingers and held the weight of her hand in mine. Her hand was warm as a river stone, brief with midday sun. In the half-light of the stained glass and the moon, her hand opened and closed. It was quiet and small against mine.

This morning on the horizon, the sun is an open violin string hung high and clear. I hang the washing because it needs to be hung.

Next to the clothesline, under the old gumtree, there's an arched barbeque area with a bricked-up wind-blocked fireplace. I was told way back when there was no lattice and the only fences here were to keep the cattle in, once-upon-a-time when my landlord wasn't a landlord, she couldn't pay the brickie for his work. One day, he turned up in the backyard with a sledgehammer in his big hands. He started swinging and didn't stop until all that was left was a pile of jagged bricks. Concrete dust hung thick like smoke in the air.

Magpies gossip and call in the branches. Black and white as a memory. As black and as white as the refusal to forget.

From behind the damp sheets, pegged tight and thin, I can hear my landlord on her phone. I grip the clothesline and wait. My fists are white, withholding. Her voice isn't the voice she uses when she talks to, or about me. It's wide and sustained, full of something I would call love. 'Alright, darling' she says, 'Nanna loves you'. Signing off With Love, Be Good.

I open one hand, release its hold. Tenants are transient, mobile things much like the chessboard shadow of a lattice fence.

And tenets are only doctrines held until, suddenly, they're not.

I open my other hand against the clothesline, freed from citrus and shadows and cleared of smoke. I hold my hands outstretched to the South Coast sky, where the space is quiet and bare and just as infinite.

Where there's nothing more to do but let go.

Transform
Kathryn Reese

The screen door rattles against its hinge,
 opening shudder suppressed by your hand.
I listen—
            you are caressing each dewdrop cradled on petal
as if contemplation alone opens flowers and wards off snails.
                What prayer!
        Nightgown and bare feet, I tiptoe out to join the dance
 the slow, careful movement—

Instead—
                this—
                    I find you
                            —shifted:
                                    Queen of the Bees
                        dress awry, thrall of drones for your
train
                You reeling
                    halfdrunk
                amongst the daisies.

Foolish, foolish girl! You have bled essence everywhere and—
    How will we ever clean this up?
 No, don't touch!
                Go sit in that corner and wait!
                                    Without touching
anything!
When I am done cleaning this
I will wipe the pollenectar from your fingers and greedymouth;
you will launder your dress and stand in the sun until it's dry.

        My child.

You have such power and such little regard.

A whole field of capeweed has been fertilised
   because of those bees.
Yes it's pretty but the crops will fail and
the milk will sour and
                  you,
                     who have not yet learned the flow
                           will likely blame the moon.
Not everything is made for your pleasure—
For your fumbling fingers to take and hold.
My child: consider the season, the wind
And the motherless swarm that now seek hive.

Drive
Kathryn Reese

I told the Queen of the Underworld to get in the back seat—
Let me drive.
She whinges, rattles salty snacks in foil packets,
Says she's bored.

I take the coast road.
There's a lookout over the cliffs—
We'll stop, I'll take her in my arms and gaze at the point where
deep meets infinite—
I want to dissolve into that place.
Be the blue that changes colour with the sun.

My Queen prefers the forest.
She knows just over the mountain—
We could lie down on our backs under the tallest tree
Shed all our significance
Let our flesh become the loam that sustains all life.

The Queen of the Underworld in the back seat of my car has
fallen silent,
Dozing or dreaming.
I wind down my window.
Let my hair dance in the salt-scented air.

Webbed
Kerry Munnery

Her name is Aggie. I didn't feel the need to call her Piscea or
Aquaria or anything like that. I knew everyone would see for
themselves what she was. My grandmother was called Agnes,
and it's a fine name.

I always thought Aggie was beautiful, whatever they said. Her
scales glint silver and mauve and pale pink as the light shifts. The
webbing between her fingers and toes is translucent. Her eyes are
shining dark, maybe a little wider, a little higher on her head than
is usual.

So after that picture went viral, I never let a laptop or even my
phone enter the room where she was sleeping. I kept out the
tornado of Tweets, the avalanche of Posts that rattled the walls of
the quiet space we made between us.

'Fish-baby' they said. 'Monster.' Claiming power over her in the
naming, like Adam.

So here is my version of the truth, for what it's worth. A mother's
truth. You won't believe it, but I don't give a fuck about that. Not
anymore.

I discovered diving after I left the Compound and the Church cut
me off from everyone I knew. My childhood friends, my parents.
I needed to fill that gap. The void where faith had been, too, if I'm
honest. You can't grow up centering your mind and body and
soul around a belief, and not feel its absence when it is puffed out
like a votive candle from one day to the next. It was no single
event, by the way, I just woke the day I turned eighteen with the
clear knowledge the life I lived was a lie. A reverse vocation, if
you like.

I had help on the 'outside.' There are people who specialise in
these things. But I was always an outsider, bewildered by
references to TV shows that had entered common use but were
alien to me, ignorant of recent geopolitical history, unknowing of
how to make friends in any normal way. At the recommendation

of my counsellor, I tried a few hobbies. Ceramics. Chess. Cooking classes. But it was when I descended into the ocean at the end of a SCUBA course that I knew I had found the answer. The blue spaces became an alternate church - quiet, mysterious, meditative. The only sound, my own breathing, slow and deep. A different kind of prayer, a different service. In the ocean I was weightless, graceful, and didn't have to speak. Angelic, I thought, hovering horizontal and motionless over the ocean floor.

Anyway, you aren't interested in all that.

The reef that particular day was something special. Ever-shifting fluid colours, like swimming inside a slowly turning kaleidoscope. Dense clouds of tiny pastel fish. I drifted away from the others and spied, almost hidden in mats of sponges and weed, a cave opening. Something pale inside. Octopus, I thought, and slipped through, expecting nothing extraordinary. But under a ceiling of stalactites, my torch showed a human face, pale and wavery, ghostlike. Before I had time to panic, to think the word corpse, to flee - it smiled. And my fear dissolved. I smiled back. That's it. I can't remember anything more. They told me I was gone half an hour, my air almost gone. They told me that when they found me and hauled me up to the boat, I fought them to get back in the water. I had to be restrained. I remember an inconsolable grief.

Gas narcosis, everyone said. Not uncommon. Once I was sensible again, I accepted the diagnosis, though the sense of loss lingered for weeks, catching me by the throat as I sat at my computer typing up endless Planning Appeals.

Perhaps I died. Everything since has been so strange that it's possible I'm in some sort of afterlife. Maybe it's you that doesn't exist.

I didn't connect the pregnancy with that incident, at first. In fact, for months I didn't even know I was pregnant at all. I had not been raised discussing the nuances of the human body. My mother, in our Church's tradition, had slapped me when I got my first period. Eventually, out of irritation at these vague symptoms of nausea and bloating, I saw a doctor to discuss food intolerances.

'Pregnant. There's your answer,' she said, holding out the test.

It took a full minute for me to get my breath. 'I can't be. I'm a virgin,' I said at last.

She was a nice doctor, but she gave me a sideways look. I learned that there's no point telling people there was no man involved. No one is going to take you seriously and start researching Immaculate Conceptions or possibilities of parthogenesis.

I had heard of abortion, but I was child enough of my parents to accept this as my miracle. In truth, I was lonely, still. The baby would be someone just for me.

Labour was hard, but followed the normal course. I groaned and sweated alone, except for midwife, until finally Aggie slipped straight out, catching us by surprise and slithering onto the mat where I squatted, so that I picked her up in my own hands. Her gills were open as she was born, but they closed up in the air, and she took a breath in the ordinary way.

'She's beautiful,' I said. What would I know about how a newborn should look?

But the midwife gaped wordlessly.

'Isn't she?' I said, faltering.

I pushed out the placenta, purple and spongy, but perhaps they are all like that.

They put her to my breast, and she latched onto me.

One of the doctors took charge, sending spectators out of the room, calling for specialists. I leaned down and sniffed Aggie's head. Salt and milk combined to create the scent of fresh blood. I gave her a discreet lick. Mine.

Only then did I count the months on my fingers, back to that day. Flashes of memory. Rough silvery-white skin under my fingers. I opened my mouth to tell someone, and shut it again. I had learned that much at least.

Masked and gowned doctors had confabs in corners. The pediatrician approached the bed and touched Aggie's gills with gloved finger, picked delicately at her scales. She talked at me with a lot of multisyllable words that ended in 'iosis' and 'axia' and 'itis'. They thought the scales must be a skin condition, though had no explanation for the gills, the webbing between her fingers and toes, the eyes. They wanted to take her away.
'No!' I said.
'Tests,' they said. 'It's normal. Usual. We'll bring her straight back.'
'No.' I wept, but they glanced at each other and pulled her gently from my arms.
I should never have let her out of my sight.

Here's a legend for you: once upon a time, no one would have considered the idea of sharing a picture of a newborn and encouraging the whole world to mock.
'Burn it with fire!' one of them said. 'Grilled or fried?' another replied. People thought that was funny. Maybe it would be, if it wasn't about this real baby I held in my arms, curling her fingers around mine.
I copped my share of comments too, being not particularly thin. Jokes about harpoons, and blubber. Illustrations of what I must have done, with what creature, to produce 'that'.
For the first time since I left the Church, I wondered if I had made the right decision. Life on the outside was proving to be full of devils after all. Social media had slipped into the role of the judgemental God –all-seeing, all-knowing, never sleeping. Holding you up for judgement, and swift punishment, if you failed to meet an ideal. The Word interpreted through gurus with unquestioning Followers.
The ones who fawned over her were almost as bad as the trolls. One of them got into the hospital room. She was all draperies and long frizzy plaits with bits of shell twined in them, wanting to 'commune' with the 'mermaid'.

'She's not a fucking mermaid,' I said, but she made a grab for Aggie and the nurse called security.

One person messaged me directly, and seemed kind. He said he wanted to hear my viewpoint. Give me a chance to put the record straight. 'Tell your own story,' he said and there was no one to warn me of the danger.

I am pretty sure I only talked to him about how we just wanted to be left alone. I did not speak about her possible conception, but I may have said something about being responsible for how she was. Something like that. I can't remember.

The day after it was all over the world again. 'Fish-baby FAKE! Mother Scars Child for Publicity!' TV Morning show presenters expressed shock, they were parents themselves. They could not imagine.

Aggie, oblivious, suckled and belched and slept and sighed. Her shit smelled like seaweed icecream left in the sun.

In a desperate moment, I tried to contact my mother. Part of me had never believed she would adhere to the ban on me after I left the Compound, and even after all these years I guess I still had hope.

'Mum?' I said. 'It's me. You have a granddaughter.'

I could hear her breathing, in and out, waves on the shore. Perhaps she was crying. Finally, she spoke. 'It is God's judgement,' she said, and hung up.

She had seen the picture, I suppose.

The Hospital had no grounds to force us to stay. They could not make up their minds what was 'wrong' with Aggie, but they determined that she was not infected or infectious, that she was otherwise healthy, whatever that might mean. I swaddled her in blankets and pulled a knitted hat down over her head scaly head and smuggled her away.

I would have taken any house that was available and remote and close to the sea, but as it happened, I loved the little cottage the first time I saw it. Square and simple but enough. A big room for cooking, eating and living, and for my bed, a little room off it for Aggie to sleep. A ramshackle bathroom lurching off the side. I painted the nursery a pale blue-green and set Aggie's shell mobile to spin slowly on its driftwood arms.

The house was set on a big overgrown block with a path from the back gate, arched in twisted ti-tree, that led to our own little cove. Rockpools held delicate blood-red sponges that shrank from our touch.

There were a few other inhabitants of the little township, who didn't want to be bothered with me any more than I did with them. People did not come to this island to be sociable, and that suited me fine.

Aggie thrived. At six months she could swim in the rockpool, paddling with her hands, kicking clumsily with her chubby little legs. She duck-dived, came up laughing with water streaming from her scales. Weighted, I descended to watch over her play. In my clumsy equipment, I envied her capacity to be so at home in the water. Her gills flapped, her fingers and toes spread, and she spiralled through the pool without effort. She grabbed at my mask, and tugged at the cold metal I breathed through, as if wondering what they were for. I had to push her hands gently away.

When we were tired, we had our supper on the rocks and watched the sun go down. Aggie loved sardines, and the seagulls squawked for the leftovers. There weren't many.

I needed to refill the air in my tank, and stock up the larder with her sardines and tinned oysters, and food for me. Toilet paper, nappy-wash. We made a careful trip on the ferry to the mainland town.

'Allergies,' I said to an overcurious waiter who caught a glimpse of Aggie's scaly face. 'Are there nuts in this?' That shut them up. On the empty next table, a headline in one of the tackier publications.

'EXCLUSIVE TV INTERVIEW! Fish-baby Grandparents To Tell All!'

I took the magazine by the tips of my fingers. It was foul, a visual assault with its exclamation marks and clashing colours and jagged shapes encasing claims to the TRUTH!

They must have offered my parents a lot of money. Not for them, for the Church. The Reverend would smack his lips at the thought of it, and permit anything.

I told myself I would not watch, but of course I could not help it. My father raved about sin, and curses, and devil's children. The presenter was clearly laughing at my oblivious parents, she could hardly contain her smirk.

'You live a secluded life. Why come out now? Why do this interview?' she said in the end, fake-hardline. 'Is it just for the money?'

'We prayed on it, and asked the Reverend for guidance. He told us that it was a way to turn spread the word, sound a warning. A way to put evil to good use.'

I stared at my mother, who had said little, looking uncomfortable but giving small nods.

'What about you, Margaret?' the presenter said at last, mock-sympathy now. 'She's your daughter. How do you feel about it all?'

My mother's mouth worked as if it was fighting all the things she wanted to say, and not-say. Finally, she spoke. I leaned forward.

'We did our best. It was she who walked away from the Light,' she said. 'But it seems I gave birth to a monster,' she said, her eyes sliding sideways. 'So, she is punished by giving birth to one too.'

I dandled Aggie on my lap, kissed her little hand. She licked my tears from her webbing. But I had other things to think about. They would know where we were, now. My parents would have sold that information too, if they were offered enough pieces of silver.

The next day on the beach I suited up, checked my equipment. I had a thin green cord which I tied around Aggie's waist, and then mine. She gazed up at me in surprise as I carried her past the rockpool to the shore where the waves lapped at the pebbly beach. It was all I could do to hold her as she wriggled and squirmed in excitement. She was always slippery. We waded out, and plunged under when it was deep enough. Aggie, ecstatic, flitted about, testing the boundaries of the bigger space around us. I was glad of the cord.

Limitless, I thought, tugged along behind her. Though not for me. She swam back and hovered in front of me. Suddenly, playfully, she snatched away the metal mouthpiece that delivered me my bottled air. This time, I did not reach to retrieve it. She held both of her webbed hands to my face and I rested mine over them as we watched the last bubbles rise. She smiled.

Nefertiti and the Nile
Jane Frank

The Goddess of Scribes I knew as a child
said if you write something down
it is more likely

to happen. I sit in the temple garden
where an offering burns to Aten.
I am one point

of the triangle, a divine one. It is now
October and floods have returned
to this lotus-shaped

valley. The green banks of date palms
and banana trees are like the soft
flesh inside a dry husk.

Egypt is the Nile's gift. When married
we were given water from the
river as a present

and I conceived quickly – six daughters –
but now my flesh is drying up.
The sun's yellow

looks untrue. I clasp an old amulet tightly
in my hand. I have tried many
times to talk to

the Sun God but perhaps there is only
a basin of water for the soul
after all?
This world we built is beautiful: rising
courtyards of grape vines, bright

flowers an earthly

cosmos. Huge sycamore-figs bring me
comfort, but perhaps scribes already
write a spell

in my funerary book. After all, he has
replaced me. A new son, not mine.
I reach the statues

of us, stretching tall as clouds, gaze up
at myself. Beauty will not help me
now, nor the high

blue headdress, nor exotic jewels, art-
works. I place the letter at his feet.
Turn my back

on all but the fast river.

Note: Soon after Pharaoh Akhenaton's twelfth regnal year, Queen Nefertiti
vanished. There is no record of her death and no evidence that she was ever
buried in the Amarna royal tomb. Her body has never been found.

Coyote Heart
Emily Paskevics

I.

In the dead of winter, the family living at the edge of the woods woke to find their chicken coop ransacked. Nothing but blood, feathers, and chicken shit was left. Coyotes, the husband spat. His wife lamented. Scavengers, marauders, thieves—coyotes killed livestock, raided gardens, and even snatched an unattended baby or two along the way.

The family's cow was unharmed, bleating in distress from the shed, but the hens and their eggs had been essential. Husband and wife conferred in hushed tones over their daughter's head. A deer would save them from starvation, they decided, providing meat for months to come.

After breakfast, the husband ventured out for an overnight hunt. The woman and her daughter cleaned up the mess the coyotes left behind. Later, they dressed for the bitter weather and headed out hand-in-hand, moving through the woods towards the local shrine.

The shrine was known as Our Lady of the Wellspring. It was little more than a narrow trickle among the stones, but the water never froze over. Our Lady belonged to a half-forgotten religion, and it was unclear whether she was a goddess or a saint, wood nymph or sprite. But it didn't matter. She was as old as the forest itself.

The woman and her daughter walked single file among the trees. Alongside her rifle, the mother carried a cask of milk they exchanged for eggs with an elderly neighbour along the way, as her daughter carried a small basket of offerings for the shrine— bread, an old deer antler, a sprig of dried rosemary.

Stamping through the snow, mother and daughter took turns calling out Our Lady's many names: Our Lady of the Good Hunt, Our Lady of Full Bellies and Stirred Pots. It was mostly about food, because in winter they were always thinking about survival. There was also Our Lady of the Tender Hearthfire, and Our Lady of Shadows on the Snow. In summer, she might be Our Lady of the Wild Berries, Leaving Stains on Our Hands. Or she might be Our Lady of the Green Language—referring to an ancient term for birdsong.

The little girl pointed to a series of canine pawprints criss-crossing the path before them. Mama, what animal made those? The woman crouched, placing her hand next to one of the tracks.

"Coyote," she said, standing and brushing snow from her knees.

"The coyote that killed the chickens?"

"Maybe," the woman said, squinting ahead.

They reached the shrine, setting their bundles next to an ancient oak—long ago, someone had carved a woman's face into its trunk. Clay pots and bunches of herbs lined the stone altar nearby. Mother and daughter knelt, drinking with cupped hands, murmuring old prayers, asking for sustenance through winter, and leaving their offerings among the rest.

Afterward, threading back through the woods, they came across the coyote prints again. On a whim, the woman took her daughter's hand and followed the tracks. She had a half-mad idea that where the coyote went, there would be food. Sure enough, the tracks led to a small clearing where she glimpsed the quivering snout of a rabbit in the snow. The woman raised her rifle. The girl squeezed her eyes shut as her mother pulled the trigger.

Before going to bed that evening, they left a small dish of fresh rabbit stew on the altar in the corner of their cabin, in gratitude to Our Lady.

The following morning, the woman ventured into the forest alone. She trailed the coyote, pausing where he had lingered, crouching to sniff where he had sniffed, noting the yellowish spray of scent markings along the way. She found scat with tufts of fur in it. After a couple of hours, the woman successfully located a plump grouse, her next prey.

Our Lady of the Secret Hunt, she murmured as she retrieved the carcass. Our Lady of Stealth and Coyote Tracks.

The woman continued to learn from the unseen coyotes. By following their tracks, she discerned where to find small game— grouse and hare, wild turkey, grey squirrel. Sometimes she brought her daughter with her, showing the girl how to move stealthily through the snow, how to distinguish rabbit tracks from a squirrel's. More often, she went alone. She hated leaving the little girl for so many hours at a time, but it was easier to hunt on her own. She gave her daughter tasks to accomplish in the intervening time: By my return, finish carding all the wool in the basket. Remember to stir the soup and keep the fire going. Milk the cow before she starts moaning.

Sometimes, sitting by the window as she mended her own stockings, the girl heard a distant shot ring out and knew her mother would be home soon with something to fill their bellies. Our Lady the Mother-Huntress. They had never felt so well-fed.

II.

One afternoon in late winter, as they hurried home from the shrine through lightly-falling snow, the little girl tugged her mother's sleeve and cried out: Mama, look!

Beneath a tamarack just off the path, a dark-furred coyote was struggling in a trap. Mama, the girl whispered. It's hurt. Trappers often passed through the region, trading meat or furs for food and a place to sleep before moving on. The woman hesitated, considering the unknown trapper's livelihood. But there was something about the look in the coyote's eyes. She stepped closer, keeping her daughter safely behind her. She narrowed her own eyes. The coyote was female, she realized, and pregnant.

The woman instructed her daughter to hide behind a nearby tree. She sang softly as she approached the coyote, her rifle hidden in her cloak. Even exhausted after hours of struggling, a trapped animal could still lunge and attack. Trappers usually shot an ensnared animal from a distance before circling in to collect the bounty.

The girl watched wide-eyed as her mother offered the coyote one of the three grey squirrels she'd shot that morning. Then, in a single motion, the woman released the snare and leapt back, aiming her rifle at the coyote's heart. The coyote only hesitated for a split second before twisting away and limping off, the squirrel dangling from her jaws. The woman re-set the trap. Thick white flakes were falling, promising to bury the evidence of what she'd done by morning.

Heading back to the cabin, the woman instructed her daughter not to tell her father about what happened. Coyotes were considered free game in the region, and releasing one—even or especially a pregnant coyote—was unpardonable.
The girl liked having a secret with her mother. Our Lady of the Secrets of the Forest, she chanted. Her mother squeezed her hand. Yes, she said. Our Lady of All Secrets Ever Kept.

III.

That night, the woman couldn't sleep. She thought of the wounded coyote, worrying about her chances of survival. Stoking the fire, the woman saw the coyote's amber eye peering at her through the flames.

The following morning, she went out to hunt alone. She moved cautiously, knowing a trapper was around. She headed deep into the forest before locating familiar canine tracks. The trail led her across the frozen river, where she followed the coyote's trail through the ravine, climbing a steep slope to an unfamiliar clearing. Crouching behind a snow-laden spruce, she watched as a pale coyote slipped into a hollow among the roots of an oak. Her breath caught in her throat. He must be the male, while the dark-furred female was somewhere within. She watched the coyote moving in and out of the den until her fingers started to stiffen with cold.

Before leaving, the woman extracted the stale heel of dark bread, potato peels, and milk she'd intended to eat for lunch. Blessing each item in the name of Our Lady, she set the scraps by the den before leaving.

But in following the coyote's trail through the ravine, she realized that she had ventured farther than usual. She started to wander, swallowing back fear, trying to re-trace her own path. A light snow was falling, already obscuring her tracks.
She said a quick prayer to Our Lady for safe passage, listening for the sound of water running under ice. If she could find the river, she could follow it partway home. Instead, she heard footsteps. Her heart jumped as a man approached. She stood still, holding her rifle in position. When his eyes finally landed on her, he started with surprise. After a strained moment, she lowered her gun. The trapper was younger than she was, tall and broad, rough around the edges.

"I came looking for coyotes, and instead I find a woman," he said, trying to be friendly. "Or are you a coyote, dressed as a woman?"

He smiled at his own joke. The woman cleared her throat. When she spoke, her voice sounded gruff, unfamiliar to her own ears.

"Which way to the river?" she asked, holding his gaze.

The trapper pointed in the direction she was already heading.

"Blessed by Our Lady," she said, the traditional farewell of those parts.

"Blessed by Our Lady," he repeated after a moment's pause.

She could tell by his hesitation that the expression was unfamiliar to him—he must've come a long way. She felt his eyes on her as she slipped away through the trees.

That evening, after dinner, the woman prepared a bath. She melted snow in a bucket by the hearth and scrubbed her daughter down. Our Lady of the Holy Waters, they chanted. Our Lady of the Melting Snow. When her daughter was dry, the woman had her turn. She washed herself tenderly, as though she hadn't touched the skin on her breasts and thighs for a long time.

Afterward, the little girl braided her mother's damp hair by candlelight. She said she wanted hair as long as her mother's, which was thick, tawny, and reached well past her hips. Her mother assured her that her hair would be even longer one day, and raven-dark, like her father's.

That night the woman dreamed of a burrow—an earthen hollow that felt womb-safe. She wasn't alone. In the darkness she sensed the warmth of fur and living breath. A man's hands were on her, his body pressing against hers, then pressing into her, in the velvety gloom.

She rolled away from her daughter, gazing into the smouldering embers in the woodstove.

IV.

After a breakfast of broth and dark bread, the woman pulled on her cloak and boots. The girl protested, wanting to go with her. The woman promised to take her the following day, but her daughter stomped her foot. Her mother spoke harshly then, scolding, and when she left the girl was still sulking.

The woman followed her familiar route through the trees. Under new snow the forest was a clean slate—all tracks were fresh. She made a quick kill of a hare, meaning she could return early to make amends with her daughter. But she didn't turn back. She headed deeper into the woods, wanting to know if the trapper had found the coyotes. Soon, she came across a man's heavy tread in the snow. Large, deep, and evenly paced—the measured footprints of a man who didn't hesitate. She started tracking him, moving swiftly through the snow. Finally, pausing to catch her breath, she heard the crunch of a footfall behind her.

The woman whirled around, and there he was. She'd been following his tracks as he followed hers, circling around and then right into each other. Her heart rabbited in her chest.

"Lost again?" he asked with a grin.

She took a step toward him. "No," she said, giving him a slow smile in return. "In truth, I was looking for you."

She followed the trapper to his makeshift camp, where he kindled a small fire. He offered her bread, she offered him milk. Then they crawled on hands and knees into his tent.

At first they removed only the necessary clothes, clumsy and rushed, trying to get everything done at once. But soon they were naked, moving and breathing in tandem. In the cabin with her husband, their daughter just across the darkened room, the woman usually smothered herself—foregoing her own pleasure. But in the woods with the trapper, she let herself writhe and moan, crying out until she was breathless.

Our Lady of the Secret Pleasures, she thought, lingering with him under the furs. Our Lady of the Coyote Heart.

In the days to come the woman continued to lure the trapper far from the coyotes' den with the subtle promise of her body. In turn, she repeatedly broke the promise to her daughter about accompanying her, knowing one secret was already too much for a child. Her daughter grew sullen.

The woman hunted, cooked, cleaned, mended, and made love with the trapper in the late afternoons. At night she paced the dark cabin as her daughter slept, fretting that the coyotes might howl, alerting the trapper to their presence. As the wind shook the eaves, the woman wanted to howl herself—to hear her own voice echoing through the snowbound silence of the woods.

V.

One morning, the woman visited the trapper's camp and found it abandoned. As she had expected, he'd moved on to set snares and traps elsewhere in that rough, remote country.

There was a wild, fleeting moment when she almost followed him. She stood knee-deep in snow, her hair loosening from its braid as the wind picked up. Then she laughed out loud—a little at herself, and at him. Her plan had worked. She circled around to the coyotes' den, where she discerned a faint mewling from within. The cubs had been born. She rejoiced. For now, they were safe.

That evening, the woman came home to find her husband waiting for her. He'd returned empty-handed from another overnight hunt. Her blood froze when he spoke.

"Tell me about the coyotes."

She turned from him, shrugging off her cloak. Her hands trembled as she met her daughter's gaze. A triumphant look darkened the little girl's eyes.

Our Lady of the Unholy Betrayal. Our Lady of the Daughter's Revenge.

VI.

The next day, the husband headed out into the bush before sunrise. When he returned in the evening, a dead coyote was strapped across his back. He dropped the carcass on the floor.

"This is how you take care of your family," he said.

The little girl started to cry. The woman reeled, grasping at the woodstove for balance. She hardly noticed as her flesh seared against the iron. When she looked down, the skin on her palm had bubbled where it burned.

That evening, her daughter massaged a salve of calendula and beeswax into her scorched hand. They didn't speak, but just before bed the girl placed three pinecones on the altar in the corner of the room. Pinecones were traditionally used to ask Our Lady for forgiveness. The woman stroked her daughter's dark hair with her good hand.

The husband skinned the coyote the following morning. He left the hide stretched across a wooden hoop to dry in the sun, and that's when the woman realized that there wasn't just one skin, but two. One was large and dark, the other was smaller and grey-white—the mother coyote and one of her cubs.

Something precious and fragile in the woman cracked. Despite the relief of spring as the new season enlivened the woods, she became listless. She stopped hunting in the woods. Her hand still hadn't fully healed when the river broke free of its icy cage, swelling its banks. The injury prevented her from performing the many chores of early spring—digging, planting, clearing, raking. Adding to her burden was the fact that she was pregnant with the trapper's son.

She visited the shrine, drinking the cold, clear water offered by Our Lady, but was unable to summon her strength. From the wellspring she called to her daughter when she wandered too far, and the girl pretended not to hear her. The woman saw in her daughter a wild restlessness that mirrored her own. She both loved and lamented this.

Later that spring, the girl made her first kill, using a crossbow to stalk and shoot a grouse. The woman showed her how to pluck and gut the bird, satisfied that her daughter was learning to take care of herself.

A few days later, the woman miscarried the trapper's son. She buried the bloody remains in the woods, along with the stained cloths—asking the old trees to take care of him, and take him back where he belonged.

VII.

The woman sat unmoving before the fire. She hadn't eaten in days. She claimed to be fasting for Our Lady, but her daughter sensed the woman's aching sorrow. She combed out her mother's braid, noting the wisps of silver around the roots.

Eventually, the girl set down the comb and went to the wall behind the bed, where her father had hung the coyote hides on display. She breathed in the pungent scent of the fur. Kneeling, she draped the larger hide around her mother's shoulders.

The woman stirred. She shifted and stretched. Her dull expression sharpened. She placed the smaller hide on the girl, who gazed up at her mother with keen amber eyes.

The woman sprang to her feet, and her daughter followed. They paced the cabin, gnashing their teeth. Throwing the door open, they fled into the late afternoon sun, yipping and howling, pawing at the ground. They broke into a trot, picking up speed until they were no longer running on two legs, but cantering on all four. Mother and daughter headed straight for the wellspring at the dark heart of the woods—side-by-side as they ran, making their way home at last.

i. Sea foam

Once upon a time, was my mother
Young and red, with jade fishtail braid.
She crossed the sea as one of four
And glimpsed a handsome world above.
How she wished to walk in their wake.
Only, to bestow upon it her love
She had her tongue cut on playground swings
The only one in the yard who sharp
-ened chopsticks not pitchforks
*"So I shall die," said the little mermaid, "and as the foam of the sea I
shall be"*

A graveyard of oversized heads
Underdrawn eyes, there lies a whisper
Of jobs stolen, people smugglers
Foreign investment digressing
From who offered the sunken ship
Of stolen treasures, bottled message
"she was very nearly turning back;
but she thought of the prince, and of the human soul
for which she longed, and her courage returned." Oh, Mama.

Why want them when you be us?
They transplanted you just young enough
That you know they're saying it wrong.
Why want them when they're your family?
You're not meant to want your family
They're meant to love loudly not tough love
"you will feel great pain, as if a sword
were passing through you. But all who see you will say that
you are the prettiest little human being they ever saw."

"If he told me he liked my almond
Eyes and caramel skin, I would tell him
To buy a bag of confection-
Ery instead." You laughed and cried when
I lent you the book I studied, but
You still say "that's so Asian"
Read: derogatory.
You still say bao/pau when I can't
Make my uncut tongue wax lyrical
Loud enough for you to love you.

Sea foam she became, cresting blue but
Never in it, evaporating
On the sand. I let you whet my palm
Be it against your oppressors
Or against your love for their boot.
You'd like me to stay dry and white with
The legs you bled for since thirteen
But your desire parted the waves
Two worlds I am left to walk between.

ii. How can I
How can I write of Athena's wit
When wit means manhood
Born from a man's brain into
Economic struggle
With a splash of virginity
Vestal or vilified.

How can I smear Hera's rage
When we Homer in
On the Grimm-tailed reality of
God forbid–Remarriage
Does she exist for cuckoldry?
To lighten the mood of Zeus
Raping, making brood?

How can I not cry in Atwood's
Penelopiad
When the highborn are silenced with
Slaved silence
When Butler's world is painfully
Fairest of them all
When my lecturer said the Big Bad
Is not wolf but man

How can I not love Homer memes
Riordan and Beowulf zines
How do I not love the pearly
Foundations of white
I long not to write of white west myth–
So open her jar
Peck me chained and blame me for war
Only then at moonrise, Artemis
Will begin the hunt.

Quotes from Anderson. H, 1837, *The Little Mermaid* & Pung. A, 2014, *Unpolished Gem*.

Amplexus
Janeen Samuel

The scene is Barbara's Beard Room. That's what she calls it, though it's no more than the curtained-off end of her caravan. She is sitting there this afternoon engaged in the endless job of repairing her stock-in-trade. Her friend the princess – ex-princess if you want to be picky – has come to help. The two of them have been working for a while in silence. The only sounds are the faint "plock" of needles passing through cambric and the thumps and cries from outside where the tumblers are practising.

The princess puts the last stitch in a long white beard, hangs it on its hook, picks up the next one in the pile. It's a neat affair in bright azure. She holds it out in front of her and makes a face at it.

"I don't know that I want to repair you. You were a nasty piece of work if ever there was one."

"Oh, I don't know." Barbara glances up, then returns her attention to the mass of red curls on her lap. "If you ask me she had only herself to blame. She shouldn't have been so nosy. Every man's entitled to keep at least one secret from his wife. And vice versa, of course." She speaks with some authority. A good many men have passed through Barbara's life at one time or another.

"That's all very well," concedes the princess, "if the secret just concerns him. But what if it affects her as well as him? If he didn't tell her before the wedding, then he married her under false pretences."

Barbara's needle halts in mid-air above the russet beard. Something in her friend's voice tells her they are no longer discussing the crimes of the legendary Bluebeard. She picks her words carefully. "Oh, I agree. In that case she'd be perfectly justified in walking out on him."

"You think so?"

"Absolutely."

Silence again. But of a different order now. Barbara bends her head over Barbarossa and stitches industriously, but in her mind all the details of the old scandal are whirling around. She remembers them well even though she wasn't, at the time, a citizen of either of the countries involved.

***

It had been the biggest royal wedding of the decade. So the abrupt departure of the bride, just two days later, from the luxury resort that was hosting the royal honeymoon, was unexpected. It was also undiplomatic. Before the absconding bride had made it back to her native land, her new father-in-law had massed his troops along the border and was threatening invasion, and the prince, her jilted bridegroom, was hastening to join him.

The princess's royal father hurriedly gathered his own troops and marched to confront the invaders. This left his palace dangerously under-guarded. The populace seized the opportunity, stormed the palace, and in an excess of revolutionary zeal slaughtered the entire royal family and the majority of its courtiers and servants.

At the frontier, the two opposing kings were killed in the fighting. The general of the defending forces, freed from royal interference, promptly led his army to a decisive victory and sent the would-be invaders fleeing. He then returned to the capital, took charge of the revolution, declared himself president of the new republic, and proceeded to pacify the populace with a program of bread and circuses.

The jilted and defeated prince returned to his own palace where he died shortly afterwards from, so it was reported, a fungal infection. The crown passed to his brother, who was popular and moderate.

As for the princess who had precipitated all this upheaval, she had taken refuge in a small neighbouring duchy. It was independent, officially neutral and extremely nervous, and as soon as order had been restored in her homeland it returned her there, politely but firmly.

The question there was what to do with her? The populace had no stomach for finishing off in cold blood what it had begun in hot. But the new President wasn't keen on having a surviving member of the Old Regime rattling around. And there was no longer a palace for her to rattle around in. The parts of it that had not been burned to the ground had been converted into a mill and factory for the production of bread, while the surrounding park and woods had been cleared, ploughed and planted to wheat.

The princess had received no training in the manufacture of daily bread. She proved however, somewhat surprisingly, to be an accomplished juggler. She was therefore assigned to the new state-subsidised circus. There she was reported to have formed a liaison with a clown and was generally believed, when anyone thought of her at all, to be living if not happily ever after at least in reasonable contentment.

"But why?" Nobody seems to have asked that at the time. There was too much else going on. These days, only children ask it – children too young to recall the events, who are being instructed in the history of their glorious republic. "Why did the she run away from the prince? What was wrong with him?"

"Never mind that," is the reply from parents and teachers. "That's not the part you need to learn." Only sometimes, the question is asked beside a winter fireside where a grandmother sits knitting, or in a drowsy summer courtyard where an old aunt is shelling peas. The reply then is different: "Aha, that was because he wasn't a normal young man at all. He'd been under a spell. You see, one day when the princess was still quite young, she was all by herself in the forest near her father's castle, playing with a golden ball beside a deep, dark well..." But as often as not the story is interrupted at this point by a cry of, "Now, mother, don't you go filling the child's head with all that old rubbish." And the tale is left untold.

The only person who knows the answer, the princess herself, has kept her own counsel. Maybe she has confided in Freddo the clown but that's the same as telling nobody. The circus people are not inclined to pry; too many of them have dark secrets in their own past. They are pleasant enough to the ex-princess but they mostly keep their distance. Only Barbara the Bearded Lady, who grew up in the duchy that briefly sheltered her, is close to being a friend. And the princess has never confided in her. Until now...

"It wasn't a well."

Barbara jumps. They have been silent so long she has assumed the subject has been dropped. Not that it can truly be said to have been raised. She says, very carefully, "People tell such stupid stories."

"It was a lake," says the princess. "A large pond, really. And the ball wasn't gold. It was just wood with gilt paint. My father would never have wasted that much gold on me. Anyway, gold balls would be much too heavy for juggling."

"True," agrees Barbara.

"I'd got a set of them made after we had this wandering juggler perform at the palace once. I thought it looked like fun. I used to practise out in the woods beside the lake because my father didn't approve."

"Trust a man for that," says Barbara. "All they think women need is cooking and sewing."

"Oh, he wouldn't have let me learn cooking! Sewing, yes, embroidery. And dancing and deportment. Definitely not juggling. I'd already got quite good at it, but this day it was windy and I dropped a ball. It went into the lake and the wind blew it right out into the middle before I could reach it. I was wondering how to get it, because I hadn't learned to swim then, when this fellow came along."

"Fellow?"

"Well, prince, it turned out, but I didn't know then. I thought he was a bit funny- looking, to be honest. He was all dressed in bright green. He said did I want my ball back and when I said yes he jumped straight in."

"No conditions?"

"How do you mean?"

"He didn't put the hard word on you or anything?"

"No, he just jumped in the lake, clothes and all, and swam out to the ball and brought it back. He was handing it to me, and dripping water and mud all over me, when my father and his men came riding up. My father made a huge fuss and carried on about how I'd be forever in his debt. Anyone would think he'd saved my life, not fetched a wooden ball."

"Maybe your father believed you might have drowned trying to fetch it yourself."

The princess snorts. "Actually, I think now it was all a set-up."

"How do you mean? He couldn't know you were going to drop the ball."

"No, but I suspect he'd sent the prince out into the forest on purpose to run across me and then he was planning to surprise us. Not that he needed to, because the whole reason the prince had come was to arrange a marriage. My father just liked intrigue for its own sake. Anyway, it worked; after all that fuss the prince didn't have much choice but to marry me."

"But what about you? Did you have a choice?"

"Not really. No."

"That's terrible." Barbara has more than once taken a man out of practical necessity but that, it seems to her, is quite a different matter.

The princess screws up her face, remembering. "I don't think I minded much. I'd always known I'd get married off to someone. I mean, that's what I was for, so far as my father was concerned. And the prince was quite nice, nicer than most of the nobles we'd had visiting. He didn't like bear-baiting or cock-fighting; he didn't even like hunting. And he didn't go carousing and drinking all the time, or fighting."

"What did he like to do?"

"Swim, mostly. He was a champion swimmer in his own country. He insisted on having me taught before the wedding. That was the only condition he made – apart from the money and politics of course, but he left most of that to his advisers. He wasn't interested in politics."

"It sounds to me," Barbara can't help commenting, "as if he wasn't interested in anything except swimming."

"No, that's not quite true. He liked singing and writing poetry. And dancing. Not ordinary dancing. He had this sort of leaping dancing he used to do when we were alone, out in the woods." She sees Barbara's eyes go to the window, to where the tumblers can still be heard at their practice. "Not quite like that. More kind of elegant. And on his toes." She sighs. "Oh, he was different, definitely. But in a nice way. Gentle. I thought we'd be happy enough."

There is silence for a minute, while the two needles ply in the red beard and the blue. Barbara is wondering how to approach the next, obvious, question.

At length she says, stretching the truth a little, "Of course it can be a shock, the honeymoon night, for a well-brought-up girl. You won't believe it but I was quite horrified my first time, when I found out what was involved. My mother hadn't told me a thing."

The princess gives a snort of laughter. "You're right, I don't believe it. But you're wrong about me. I knew all about it. Nanny had told me."

"Nanny?"

"She was my nurse. My wet-nurse. They sent her away when I was five, but I used to sneak off and visit her. Her husband had been a woodsman, only he died. She had a little hut in the forest. She taught me nearly all the useful things I ever learned. But it wasn't just her. She had a son – he would have been my foster-brother only they hadn't let her bring him to the palace. She had to leave him at home with his big sister, who wasn't really old enough to look after him, and one day he got too near the fire and set himself alight. He was terribly scarred and he never learned to talk; Nanny said that was the shock. But he liked me. When I was out by the lake he'd sometimes bring me presents. Little things – flowers or berries or things he'd carved. We got to be fond of each other. And then... Well, Nanny had given me the theory, but it was with him I learned the practice." She paused, gazing at the blue beard as if into a lost forest glade. "We knew it couldn't last. We were both realists. What I mean is, I'd never expected it to be quite like that with the prince. But all the same..."

"He didn't measure up?"

"Measure up! Listen, the first night, he lay on his side of the bed and went fast asleep. And I thought, well, it had been a very long day and we were both tired, so fair enough. I thought perhaps in the morning... But no, when I woke up he was already out of bed and doing laps in the pool. So then I thought, all right, tonight's the night."

"And was it?"

"It was the night all right. After we'd had our candle-lit dinner and he'd said a few poems and sung me a song or two, he said why didn't we go down to the pool in the moonlight? He seemed a bit excited by then so I said fine and off we went, and we took off all our clothes and went in naked. It was pretty romantic – nice warm water, moon and stars overhead, you can imagine."

There is a long pause. Barbara tries to be patient. But it's too much for her.

"And then?"

"And then he came up behind me, clasped me round the waist and started squeezing me in and out."

"And...?"

"And nothing. That was it. It seemed to be giving him a lot of pleasure, but it wasn't doing much for me. If I tried to turn round he just hung on harder. I tried reaching my hands back towards him but he just yelled, 'Paddle with your hands. Paddle.' In the end he let go, climbed out of the water and pulled me out after him. He patted me on the cheek, said, 'Good girl,' and hopped off to bed and fell straight asleep. That's when I started packing."

"I don't blame you," says Barbara. There is a word trying to pop into her head. Her native duchy believes in giving its children a good all-round education and the one subject she enjoyed at school was Natural Science.

"Amplexus!"

"What?"

"Amplexus." Already Barbara's wishing she hadn't spoken. "It doesn't matter. Just, it's the way frogs do it. Not like proper mating, it all happens externally."

The princess looks totally blank. "Frogs? What...?"

A stick rattles along the side of the caravan and a boy's voice calls, "One hour to performance time." They've been so engrossed they didn't hear him coming.

Barbara gives a squawk of relief which she manages to turn into alarm. "Help! I didn't realise it was so late. I've just got Barbarossa finished in time."

A minute later she stands at her window, still clutching the red beard, and watches the princess hurrying back to her own caravan. Inside it Freddo, the clown who never speaks, will be getting into his costume and applying the thick greasepaint that transforms his scarred face. Maybe, thinks Barbara, it is a fairy story after all, and the princess is living happily ever after.

A tear drops onto the russet curls of the Barbary pirate and lies there like a pearl. Then Barbara shakes herself and begins to dress for her performance.

Wild and Tangled
Sarah Temporal

Under a powder-blue sky with drifting smoke   there's a back
road that no one has cause to take   A fence with leafless
rosebushes   skulls of steers guard the gate   The house is
ringed with rambling sheds   where heavy, sharp, and
grinding tools are kept   A garden wild and tangled, flecked
with flight of red-capped fairy wrens   And you have heard:
here lives the beast.

He has such shining fur, such shining eyes   so diamond-sharp
and pale   You think you've never seen anything so male
Everybody wants to touch him   shygirls-oldwomen-
straightmen, everyone   wants to tangle handfuls of that mane
Those gleaming claws appeared no more   than fine, articulate
fingers   The way he looked at you and saw   the blood that
beat beneath your skin   seemed evidence of grace   All you
want to do is follow   every rippling cloud across his face
Wrap yourself in muscle   Sleep on growling chest   And
you think   you are the only woman   who's tucked herself
into his house   drunk the beer he handed you and thought,
'He is my life now,'   with quiet thrill.

You don't believe a thing they say in town   Besides, those
shunning only serve to harden   beastly natures of their own
And look: how he has time for all of them   Lavishes feasts of
smile and wit   Makes angelic visitations   Spreads his
redolent length upon the verandas of the lonely   You don't
need anyone else   He is huge   enough to make up for your
smallness   He protects you   and you are scared.

The dream is to reveal   what he is hiding under clothes
Perhaps the good man he grows to be   Perhaps rank pelt
wafts of sweet manure, sticky burrs, sweat and fear   It's you
alone can lick and soothe and clean away that fear   Your roots
hold fast   You weather droughts   with your wordless
friends   They flit about, the little wrens   with drops of
blood bright on their heads   You're nothing like those other
women who he tore apart   For you have read the story
Transformation at its heart   where beast is human   and
human, beast.

Then it is only a sign of intimacy and trust   to hear at night
The cries of swallows in his garden, crushed   whose nests he
batted down with thwacking paws   The cries of cattle whose
sides he slashed   and left a bloody feast for flies   Or the
cries of wallaby whose graceful necks he snapped   dragged
hot fur on the forest floor   And the rumours of women   to
whom he did all of this   and more.

I do not mean to say that nature cannot change   I saw you
stray   on that road, the stones obscured utterly with bracken
Where his scent lay thick with spreading, powerful warmth
And it is far, far too easy to say   that we must simply know
our value   refuse to be his prey   You would not be called
away   Nor should the burden of that choice be yours
Perhaps his transformation is only ever wrought   beneath the
teeth of other beasts   their particular smoke-and-fire talk
Not by all the heroic strength with which   you followed his
twitching tail   into the scrub

                              escorted by flashing reptiles and

                    the startled flight of birds.

Collecting Lemons
Jan Napier

The milk you pour, my cup ignored, is no colder
than your eyes nor the silence you're careful to keep
between us. I go out into a lesser chill.

Long grasses are unweaponed with wet, green blades
drooping to brush boots darker. Dew soaks slowly
into leather, and absorbing words we freed last night,
I feel thinned as tendrils of mist wind is lifting from river

 and eucalypts, patches of blue showing through
like an answered prayer, wish that everything so sacred
could last. Better sense tells me love's a tale that ends,
like sleep or reverie.

A puff of mud rises from under a sunken log,
nimbus of silt drifting down stream. A fish, or frog,
is hiding, or dying, or just getting on with whatever
it does, softness a secret it keeps till the moon's too much.

 I slide between fence wires, barbs snag skin, and so
simply I lose another piece of myself.
My old mare steps to ask if perhaps there's an apple

but she's happy with a pat. I lighten, smile a little, see
the world still holds tenderness, turn towards the house.

Crossing the yard I pause to collect lemons bright
as hopes I once thought would grow, these and the open
gate, all the forgiveness I have to carry back to you.

Ox-blood red
Rachel Flynn

We arrived just five minutes late, Nicola and I, walking in to the sound of the Skye Boat Song, dripping onto the carpet, not even a hand-out with the order of service left. There were hardly any seats either, so we sat separately, Nicola in the row in front of me, one seat to the left. I looked around at Marko's current friends and relatives, grey hair, hunched shoulders, paunches stretching their shirts. I sat up straighter and pulled my stomach in. We knew him from the old days. I had to lean forward to whisper to Nicola.

'Remember the time we drove from Ballarat to Nhill just to get a vanilla slice?'

'Sh!' was all I got for an answer.

Of course, she remembered. That's why she wanted to come, surely. But not a word was mentioned on the drive up.

'You and me in the back seat of Marko's Torana?' I pressed my hand to my chest. 'Marko driving and Soapy running the tape deck?'

'Sh!'

'What was Soapy's real name, do you remember?'

'Simon,' Nicola half-turned back to me. 'Now shut up.'

Simon, that's right. As if I could forget. I tried for long enough. I wondered if he was here. I looked around the room. There were plenty of retired gentlemen.

Nicola and I attended a few funerals these days. Some of our generation were trudging off a bit early, setting a trend, leading us into the curve. We only needed one outfit each. Mine was a layered range of blacks and purples, suitable for the mature woman with a soft figure. Nicola's was all blues and greens, a sharp cut with lapels and shoulder pads. Dark of course, powerful and threatening. People stood aside to let her through and I followed in her wake.

It was just luck that we found Marko making his exit, and a mystery to discover he'd reached respectability, especially as we knew where he'd come from – he and Soapy in their hotted-up Torana.

I thought back to that day we went to Nhill and an image of the two of them came to me. We were halfway there, cruising slowly through Stawell. Marko was driving with two fingers on the steering wheel and his elbow out the window. My view was of the back of his neck with his gold chain winking back the sunlight, his rusty hair curling over it in places. Then came the ribbed neckline of his blue t-shirt. I could see the seams running along his shoulders, but the rest of his outfit remained invisible to me. I knew he was wearing pale blue jeans and black thongs. Both of them were. Soapy's t-shirt was faded orange with 1970 printed on the front in fat white numerals. It way past 1970 by then, but he still had the shirt. He was fiddling with the tape deck, playing Travelling Band, as if it was midnight and they were roadies. Meanwhile Nicola was beside me in the back seat humming tunes that would become Beatles classics. Her hair was blowing all over the place due to the open window.

Soapy turned around to us and said, 'How about we pull over for a break, girls? There's a creek up here. Stretch the legs, eh? Go for a bit of a walk.'

Sure, we said. Fine. That's what girls did in those days. We rode in the back seat. Stopped when the boys stopped. Started when they started. Ate what they ate when they ate it. Got out for a bit of a walk when they wanted to. And said sure and fine and okey-dokey.

Soapy turned to Marko. 'Lemonade or cola?'

Turned out it was a reference to our hair colour, Nicola's a long pale blonde and mine dark brown

'Lemonade,' Marko said, and that's how Nicola came to be his "date", and I came to be Soapy's.

Suddenly everyone stood up. I did too, only half a beat behind them. It was time for a hymn. They all had the booklet, but not

Nicola or me. I sang along with the gent standing next to me. Could he be Soapy? Would it be too much of a coincidence to come all this way and actually find him beside me in a funeral facility? I took a punt.

'Simon?'

He turned to me like a dog does when you call his name. He nodded slightly with one eyebrow raised.

'It's Deborah,' I said.

He frowned, but kept looking at my face and hair. It was closer to pink champagne than cola these days.

'Debs,' I said. 'Hello Soapy.'

I saw then that he remembered me. A slight straightening of his back, a grimace as he looked away. A sideways look back at me, trying to see any familiarity.

'We've all aged,' I said. 'Or died!'

He nodded.

We were up to the bit where the minister makes a few guesses at the personality of the corpse – charming, a family man, a community man, a professional man, a sportsman, a staunch member of the Richmond football club, a loved husband, father and grandfather.

Yep, I thought, he'd be all of that for sure. I leant forward to Nicola.

'Is that his wife? Straight across. See? All in black. Is that her?'

'Probably,' said Nicola.

'Soapy's here beside me,' I whispered.

At last she turned around. I tilted my head slightly to my right. 'He can sing hymns now.'

Nicola gave him a severe stare, then turned to the front. I saw Soapy's adams apple bob up and down, but he kept his face blank.

It wasn't blank that day we turned off the highway and up a dirt track to the creek. We all got out for a pee. Nicola and I went to the left in among the bushes and Marko and Soapy to the right, up against the shiny trunk of a silver gum. Like dogs marking their territory. Turns out we were included in their territory, among their possessions. They had the Torana with a cassette player, a tank full of petrol and ten dollars each in their back pockets. And they had us – stupid, naive country girls.

They opened the boot, pulled out a couple of long necks from the esky, grabbed a rolled picnic blanket each and escorted us into the bush. Marko and Nicola went to the right and Soapy and me to the left, for a bit of privacy, he said. Even then I didn't twig what was going on. Maybe a bit of pashing I thought. I was up for that much.

The celebration of Marko's life was practically over. I imagined him lying inside the coffin, his blue t-shirt rolled up for a pillow, his rusty hair curling down the back of his neck, his gold chain still winking in the dark. I could see the coffin through the crowd, a pile of flowers sacrificed to his memory. It was on a trolley with wheels so there was no need for six strong men to hoist it onto their shoulders. Instead, three men stood along each side, his brothers, sons and a son-in-law, I'd say. They took up their positions ready to wheel it out. Someone went out to call the piper back. He threw his butt onto the gravel and stamped on it, then led the procession with Going Home. His kilt swished to and fro as he walked. Marko was more subdued now than on our trip to Nhill.

He and Soapy thought it was just a bit of fun, that we were up for it. Otherwise, why did we come?

We'd been lying on the blanket for a while, kissing, just kissing, Soapy and me, then he got a bit more insistent. Turns out he thought I was easy. It was the fashion at the time to wear a short cotton dress over minimum underwear. That's all Nicola and I were wearing. With platform sandals of course. Everything else was in our fringed tote bags: a hairbrush, Miss Melbourne coral lipstick, a hankie, a coin purse, a packet of Tampax and Coppertone suntan lotion. There were no mobile phones then, no

GPS, no emergency call numbers, no plastic bottles of spring water. We didn't even have hats.

Afterwards I was in tears, but not Nicola.

'Is this a double date?' she said. 'We still want that vanilla slice, don't we Debs? Are we going to Nhill or not?'

Marko shrugged. 'Yeah, that's what this is, a double date, and we are going to Nhill, and we are getting that vanilla slice.'

Soapy said nothing. He put his hand to his face where there was double red welt running from his right eyebrow to his chin. I know now that I would have had quite a bit of forensic evidence under my fingernails, but back then I was just keen to wash my hands and face in the creek. We all got back into the car. Marko put his foot down, just to see how fast that Torana would go. There was no more humming from Nicola.

Now here we were at Marko's post funeral afternoon tea. It was all very stylish. We had a lovely view of the lake and the birdlife. I got myself a cup of tea and three neat triangular sandwiches. I found a spot at a table near the doorway and ate slowly, keeping one eye on two wattle birds hanging upside down in the banksias. I kept my other eye on Soapy. He was looking very uncomfortable, running his finger around inside his collar, stretching his neck away from the knot of his tie. His wife stood beside him, patting his arm, perhaps thinking him grieving for his dead friend.

Nicola was already introducing herself to the widow. I could see her across the room, imposing in her angular suit and high heels. Her lemonade hair was now a neat clipped bob, stiff with spray. I could see she had the wife's attention, her mouth open in silent horror. One of her grown sons slid an arm around her, the look of Marko about him except for the sunglasses worn high on his forehead.

Across the room Soapy was greeting all their mutual friends, shaking hands with the men, kissing all the women, glancing across to me occasionally. Suddenly he found some courage and ushered his wife over. I stood up as they approached.

'This is Deborah,' said Soapy. 'She was at uni with Marko and me. Debs, this is my wife, Birdie.'

I smiled at her. 'It's lovely to meet you,' I said.

Soapy melted away and left us chatting. Well, that's what I wanted, so I thought.

'Simon has often spoken about you,' said Birdie. 'About the escapades you all got up to.'

'Has he?' I said.

'It all sounded great fun, those uni years. Something I always regret missing out on.'

'It was fun,' I said, 'most of it, for most of the time anyway.'

'I've heard all of the stories about those boys and their orange Torana.'

'Perhaps not quite all of them,' I said.

She nodded, expecting a story now.

'Have you heard about the trip to Nhill, just to get a vanilla slice?'

'I have,' she said. 'That's where he got the scar isn't it? The one down his face.'

'It is,' I said. 'Did he tell you how he got it?'

As soon as I said that the memory came straight back to me like it was yesterday, as well as the nausea, the heart racing, the trembling. There I was with Soapy pinning me down with his left arm across my throat, his right hand working at his fly and me with only my fingernails for protection. It didn't stop him though, that double gouge down his face. Might have made him rougher and quicker. That's all. But he's had that scar to look at every day in the mirror.

I came back to the present when I felt Birdie grasp my hand.

'Are you all right?' she said. 'You're very pale.'

She sat me down at the table where my tea had cooled.

'You stay there. I'll get you another cuppa.'

I looked back at the wattle birds. There were three now, squabbling over the flowers. I heard a pied currawong call and saw a flash of its white undertail as it launched into flight.

Birdie came back with two cups of hot tea and sat across from me.

'Simon told me about the thick bush you all struggled through and the branch slapping him in the face.'

I looked at her. She was a sad sort of woman, care-worn I'd say, probably having trouble with her grown children.

'You've had some difficulties,' I said.

She teared up then, not such a bad look at a funeral.

'I have,' she said. She pulled a tissue out from her sleeve and wiped her eyes. 'We have, I should say. Our boys …'

I could imagine it: drugs, dropping out, unemployed, broke, abandoned grandchildren - the usual demons. They've cleaned her out I suppose – money and emotions. Add that to thirty odd years with Soapy.

I nodded. 'I have boys as well.'

'But tell me about that trip,' she said, 'about going to Nhill that day.'

I hesitated.

'Go on,' she said. 'I'd like to hear about it. See if it matches Simon's story.' She raised her eyebrows at that point.

'Well. Poor Simon,' I said. 'That welt down his face must have hurt. It was swollen, and red, probably full of bacteria. Looked like a wild animal had scratched him. Must have been throbbing. Of course, there was no first aid in those days, not in that Torana of Marko's, or in our tote bags. We didn't even have a band-aid between us.'

Birdie nodded. I went on.

'Still, we kept going on to Nhill. They were good like that, those two, Marko and Soapy. If they had a plan they followed it through.' I paused here, thinking again of their plan that day. 'And that bakery in Nhill was famous for their vanilla slices at the time.'

Birdie had listened carefully. I hadn't told any lies.

'He never eats them now,' she said. 'Can't stomach them.'

I saw Nicola coming over to me. She was finished with this funeral.

'Come on Debs,' she said.

We got as far as the door and I turned back for a look. Birdie gave me a little wave. Soapy came up behind her and slipped an arm around her waist, startling her, probably wondering what I'd told her. She might have been wondering what I hadn't told her.

Before we set off Nicola checked herself in the rear-view mirror. She found a hair out of place and slipped it behind her ear. She applied some lipstick, ox-blood red these days. During the trip home she hummed along to her iPod. I gazed through the windscreen. The purple clouds had moved to the east. Nicola stared at the road ahead, then turned slightly towards me. Her features had softened. That line between her brows had smoothed out. The corners of her mouth had relaxed.

'Did you tell her?' she said.

'No,' I said. 'But she knows there's something I haven't told her.'

'You're too soft.'

'Yeah? Maybe just too subtle. Soapy will have to tip-toe around for a few years yet.'

The sun had broken out all over us. We were heading back to our daily lives of family, work, friends. I thought of my boys, working men now, all tradies of one sort or another. I thought of my husband, having to take the brunt of my experience with Soapie all these years.

I looked at Nicola. There was no one else on her list. That was it. All those names crossed out. No more revenge trips. Closure they call it. Resolution. Done. Finished.

In which Miranda returns to her island
Verity Laughton

I sat beside the water, and I saw
the sleek form of an ibis fly unskyed
where by rights I should have seen the
glassy fishes glide, or crablings hide
their dainty, armoured bodies in serrated rocks.

Perhaps it was a simple trick of water,
sun and sky. Perhaps in the vault above
where true birds truly fly, a long-necked
creature surfed between earth and heaven.
But I saw no bird. Yet I heard, bell-like
in that air, sound, not music but unexpected
harmony, a call? And I remembered
that this is a place where a bird might fly
in water, or the earth sing, or the tide
belch a concentration of oddball riddlings,
only to return them, via the world's
convection, to the massy deep where
unlit enigmas prowl the ocean floor,
and buried stars can shift a little in
a floating core, and thus unleash a storm.

And I remembered my father, walking
on this shore. And I remembered how
he talked to airy nothing, and I laughed
to see nothing in that air. Yet he talked,
and then a moment came when nothing
seemed to hang weightless between nothing,
or perhaps the nothing spoke unheard,
or perhaps the still air simply winked at nothing?

And the moment slipped, only to catch itself
before it slipped, and something was accomplished,

or replaced, and it seemed that what I knew
was no longer what I knew, or what I knew
was nothing.

I saw the bird fly, and I thought: there is
a kind of man who can see how nothing
can be everything. There is a kind of man
who speaks to both nothing, and the burning
in the deep. There is a kind of man who might,
if he chose, fly like a bird where no birds fly.
And I looked, and there in the water crawled
a blue and golden, small, efficient star
quietly consuming the life that breeds
in the shallows. I turned. I felt the blue
bewildered brightness shrug away. Day tumbled
into dusk. I leant towards the smoky light
that, shifting, slid ahead of me, and I
wondered whether magic has always been
a simple exchange of forces, whereby
what is not becomes what is, by a change
in the quality of attention?

BRCA (according to the Pythia)
Emily Tsokos Purtill

Return to the land of your ancestors
in the chalky marble dust of history
but first you must understand that
the Morai has already decided it all
karkinos does not make exceptions
for mothers
or brides clutching bracelets threaded with cloves
time folds in on itself here
you do not get special treatment
two or three generations later
your body has never left the village nor the island
you may have spent your days on the other side of this warming
planet
but the dye was cast
in all its shades of bloody crimson
long before your birth

it didn't start with you
and this is how it has always been
you can learn anything you like on the outside
be decorated with gilded letters after your name
but inside you are still a blessed/burdened woman
from that village on that island
with all its smoky rituals

only now there is a choice
if you can call it that
of scooping out flesh and tissue and cells
excising all those problematic parts
all that which makes you female
so you lie on that cold table
and count backwards from ten
you won't remember

but your body will bear the white scars of the scalpel's kiss

it is not yet time to boil wheat for your *koliva*
it is a re-routing of your path
temporarily of course
you may become a Yiayia in black
with spells on your lips

so return to your island
where the octopus tentacles are stretched and beaten
hung out in the sun
then served with salt and lemon

where nothing changes
except for the patterns in the coffee cups
but even those are not as unique as you want them to be

there have been so many of you
even if you don't recall all your lives
all those who came before
and those who will come after
you are a link in a chain
that you will never see the end of

but really
in exchange for your flesh and problematic parts
you have a length of longer thread
Atropos still holds the sharpened scissors
and she will make the cut
one day
it is inevitable
you are mortal

Return to the Labyrinth
Emma Darcy

The isle is overgrown and sleepy, the air is thick and lush and syrupy as honey with the scent of wildflowers. Tangles of grass and vines that reach to the knees snip-snap around the ankles with every step. The fat and lazy partridges which once tormented Daidalos to madness coo and chirp from the safety of nearby thickets. The sun is already beginning its descent when I arrive but there is no question of making camp under this admittedly intoxicating hammered bronze sky.

The labyrinth is underground. The entrance, when I find it, is little more than a gash in the rock. All but invisible if approached from the wrong direction or at the wrong time of day. Even knowing the portal's exact location, having had the instructions repeated to me so often I chanted them in my sleep, I still groped the craggy surface in doubt. Peered through the narrow aperture in disbelief. How could my body fit through such a narrow crack?

It was an illusion, of course, as are so many of the old inventor's ploys. It was the angle that was the key; to slip in sideways as if between two parallel planks of wood. I left the world of man and sky and grass behind me, soft and green and sweet, and followed my feet down into the gloom and the sandstone whorls of the world of the Minotaur.

I never met Minos or Pasiphae, but my mother did. It seems almost impossible to imagine that the rulers to whom she had been in service who were so known for their fairness and wisdom had anything in common with the people who were so tormented by pride, by lust, by loathing, that this place-and the creature who lived here-came to be. Daidalos did a good job. He may have loved the inner workings of things but he had an artist's eye that loved the outer shape. For all the ugliness of its function, the labyrinth is beautiful. I wonder if it was for Asterios' benefit, as the captive audience he was the one who spent the most time with these walls. Or was it for those doomed fourteen

Athenian youths who would experience it each sacrifice only fleetingly before the end?

Right inside the door, at my feet, is an old brown stain which disappears in a long smear into the shadows. I shiver, and imagine what it would be like to be taken the moment I stepped through the door while the others fled wailing into the tangled vine tunnels. I wonder if such a fate was worse-or better? I am so distracted by the patch of blood that I almost miss the long strand of thread half-buried in the dirt. I kneel down and touch it gingerly with my finger. It is tied at one end to the base of a trident which represents Minos' fidelity to Poseidon. One end of the clew that Diadalos gave Theseus to navigate the labyrinth. Well, to be accurate, Diadalos gave it to Ariadne, who gave it to Theseus. Obligation and if not love, then fondness, surely. Obligation and familiarity. The bond that is your own word, and wanting someone you think well of to think well of you.

I can't help but think that if Minos had made the sacrifice asked of him in the first place, less sacrifices would have been demanded of others later on. There are three stories here which begin with the love of a bull. Not including Europa, I suppose, but how far back in this do we go? Minos judged Pasiphae too harshly, I think, as I study the trident. After all, Poseidon gave him the bull to sacrifice and he couldn't do it, as weak for the beast's flesh as she was soon to be. The Gods are all about ironic punishments. Minos kept that bull to breed, and breed it did; a princely calf if ever there was one. And don't they always say, be careful what you wish for? Now Pasiphae, once the fire in her loins had cooled, could see she had been used. Could Minos see he had been tested, and failed? I try to imagine the moment, after the madness, exhausted and sore, as the realisation took hold of what she had done; but I've never wanted beyond all reason. I've never been seduced by a God. I cannot imagine what it is to be Pasiphae.

I like to imagine Daidolos, surrounded by harmless little partridges, convinced they are the returned soul of the protegé he murdered in a jealous rage. He has hidden them everywhere in the labyrinth, why? To show him, ha! See, I have achieved a marvel even you could never have hoped to construct? A marvel a cruelty, the boy would have shrank from, perhaps. But an undeniable wonder nonetheless. Or was he hoping to imprison the boys' ghost here, among these endless twists and turns? To kill two birds with one stone, so to speak, and dispose of both his and Minos' dirty secrets at once. But was his guilt like the twine he gave Theseus to follow out? As long as his memory, and wherever he may go, the end remained fastened.

I follow the string now in the gloom, kicking up puff after puff of dust with each step, holding my lantern away from my eyes. It winds this way and that, and so do my thoughts. I think of my mother, coming down here as a girl even younger than I am now to bring the Minotaur his meat. Asterios. She always called him Asterios. Fed from childhood on human meat. Milk, before that. Yes, milk; like any other babe.

Not Pasiphae's, of course. A wet nurse who lived with him a year while the labyrinth was being built. Maybe she loved him, a little, enough to sew his clothes and make him a single toy that my mother said he kept a long time in secret. Only she knew where it was. Because only she knew where he slept.

I thought this part was disgusting for a long time, and maybe I still don't really understand it. I try to imagine being my mother. Terrified. Her hands full of the bloody meat of- who? Beggars? Prisoners? Slaves? Standing in front of Asterios as he touched her face with a hand that was too human.

I try to imagine being Asterios, alone all the time but for the trembling girl who sneaks in to bring my meat and I have so much rage and loneliness inside me but I reach out a hand and I try so hard to touch her face gently. Maybe the first time I knock her to the floor and she screams and runs and it takes me a long time to convince her to let me try to touch her again. Maybe she has to show me how to do it. Maybe I never manage to do it without hurting her but she can tell how hard I'm trying.

She said his body was no different to a man's, powerfully built, it was just his head that was like a bull's. No bull eats meat, she would say scornfully, wiping at her eyes. Men eat meat. His eyes were of a gentle beast, tormented beyond its limits. My mother found hers too young, and I found mine even younger than her.

Theseus wasn't to know, she said, all anyone had ever been told was that the Minotaur in the labyrinth was a monster. I wonder. Theseus had fought great beasts before, and he is known as being fair and wise. So how, fighting barehanded at such close quarters, could he not see Asterios was different? But, perhaps, after two sacrifices of fourteen Athenian boys and fourteen Athenian girls, it didn't matter. What he really wanted to do was end Minos' hold over Athens. No more Minotaur, no more sacrifices. He defeated him, easily. No club, no spear. Just his demi-god hands against the pain and fear of a cow-eyed bull raised in the dark. Asterios never felt the grass underneath his feet or chewed rampion. He never felt bees buzz past his head or dug his fingers on soft dirt to the knuckle. And he only met two people in his entire life who didn't loathe him.

I wonder when, if ever, someone like Theseus finds their limits.

I found his body after some indeterminate time. I was walking, thinking my thoughts, until I saw the bones, so I stopped. I don't know what I thought. Maybe I thought after Theseus came out they would at least come in and look at him. See for themselves. Bury him.

I can see the humble bedroll on the floor in the gloom against the wall and I think 'Ah yes. Theseus the hero, defeating the dread beast as he struggles to stand from his bed'. On the wall above the bedroll there is a beautiful mural painted. My mother never said anything about it. She always thought he'd chosen a strange place to camp, but I can see why he liked it. The city is tucked away on one side and most of it is of an immense orchard overrun by people dancing and playing musical instruments among the trees. It must be of a festival, but mother never taught me about the festivals. She said they were fun and games now but almost all of them began with the murders of girls like us.

I open my bag and kneel beside the bones which even now are intimidating in their size and shape.

"Asterios," I begin, and falter. I don't like the tone of my voice, the way I yelp so loudly. "Father," I try again, "You don't know me, but I have come a long way so that you may meet me, and hear your daughter's name.

When my mother found out she was pregnant with me she went to Pasiphae, hoping. Hoping for what, I don't know. Understanding. Compassion. Kindness. Perhaps all of those things, or none of them, are why Pasiphae insisted she flee. She could have had us killed, couldn't she? Was that a kindness? Was it compassion that kept us out of the labyrinth, away from you, but free to enjoy the sun and the grass and mother's fingers on my fur, instead of yours?

"I'm sorry. I took her from you." I fall silent. My nose is wet, a feeling I hate. It has a gold hoop through it which a boy, trying to be cruel, once told me was pretty. I have since decided that it is true. The ring was a gift, at once a compliment and an insult, from my grandmother on my sixteenth birthday. A nod to my noble lineage. Best not to ask how I'd come by the iron one it replaced. That is a tale for another time.

"I brought you gifts," I choke out, and rummage in my bag. I am embarrassed that I had come so far and almost forgotten.

"Grass. It's fresh from outside. One of mother's dresses. It smells like her. I have one too, at home. Shells, from the beach. Do you hear them? I left with nothing but the dress, but on the way here I kept seeing things and thinking 'but he never saw'-oh! Bird feathers, all different kinds. There are more birds in the world than partridges. This is just a rock, but it's such a nice smooth one. I just like it. Would you mind if I kept it? Actually I..."

I had just remembered what was under the bedroll. I climbed to my feet, and left my meagre offerings piled by the enormous bones. I stepped around the makeshift altar and knelt by the bedroll instead and felt around underneath in the dirt. I found it, pressed up against the wall. It was pathetic really. Filthy and worn, carved out of wood at the head, the body and limbs were held together with pins. The little cow boy wore a grubby sack-cloth smock. I pressed it to my chest and sighed. I took it over to him and tucked it with the rest of my gifts as close as I dared get- I'd never touched a bone before.

"My name is Boba," I cleared my throat, my voice barely seemed to fill even this narrow space, just another tunnel in the labyrinth. "And there are at least three people who love you. I know that doesn't make up for everything else, but I hope it helps."

And I Suppose Poems Could Be Miniature Rooms
(each time you begin with the hope of creation)
Wes Lee

For Marty Goddard

I do remember the peace I had once
going back home to visit,
sitting in the chair I always sat in, and everything moved
as it should in the vale of peace where time had stopped.
And there was a low-key feeling of pleasure in my body.
And the sadness of realisation: *Why couldn't it always be like this?*

And this realisation happened at the time,
not after when I had left,
which is usually the case.
A strange long moment like
billions of years of time compressed.
Like a river that wobbles and seems to stop moving in the same
direction.

The moment was like a door in a doll's house opened
and a light shining out,
and all the other doors open to dark rooms where things
happened,
where things are still happening.

And I read about a woman activist
who made miniature rooms in the evenings:
dioramas portraying a mother and children;
each room lit with a tiny lampshade.
Until her whole apartment was filled.

The woman activist invented the rape kit.
A cardboard box containing a pencil, a comb, a forensic list,
swabs

and slides.
It was said she became a 'furious alcoholic'.
She alienated friends and family in the last months of her life.
It was said she withdrew, surrounded by the miniature model rooms
she loved to build.
It was said she vanished, shrinking down to nothing.
It was said she asked that her ashes be thrown to the winds
in Sedona, Arizona, along the red cliffs.
Old friends didn't even know she was gone.

But the rape kit survives.

And I think of the untested rape kits, abandoned,
warehoused, eaten by rats, mouldering under leaky ceilings.
Thousands upon thousands of minutes of pain,
of unimaginable terror
left to waste.

And the rooms she made with leadlight windows and painted
French doors;
a lily pond;
a faraway gaze.
These perfect oases of domesticity,
everything calm.

After 'The Rape Kit's Secret History' by Pagan Kennedy, New York Times

(M)other Writer
Natalie Damjanovich-Napoleon

I became an invisible writer,
hiding in closets to scribe the labor,
floating dry, ink staining the bathtub.
I cradle wobbly words beside my
newborn's unstable head
on the breastfeeding pillow.
I scratch at my book in the hallway,
tripping over my words, child at my feet.
I tap into my phone in the glow of blue light
under the invisible forcefield
of the blanket on the couch.
I play hide and seek,
scribbling in the space between
the back fence and garden shed.
A sacred workspace in my car,
my son at T-ball practice,
a cone of silence.
McDonald's has free Wi-Fi
and a playground. The pantry
at home becomes a cave
with supplies and quietude,
opening up time and space
to infinity.
Writing noise out of daycare,
preschool and school pick ups.

I have two dissertations in the circular
work of being a writer, cook, cleaner,
student, tutor, teacher, mother, farm-worker,
household manager; in having no boundaries,
losing sleep, nearly drowning,
staying up to write
until the light across the road

in front of the church goes out.

The carved hardwood desk, the view of lilting trees,
filtered light, a wife to bring me sandwiches and tea,
to keep the children at bay so I could write
Other Lies of Great Male Authors and
Writing in a Secluded Cabin in the Woods—
from my walk-in pantry. Aghast with the romance
of the twilight space I create to write my histories;
The Road Out of the Dark of Winter,
Absolving Myself of (M)other-Writer Guilt and
Holding the Thorns Back on the Path, all this work,
all this brushing away of sand for those
who come after me to be seen.

The fall of Zeus
Rachael Mead

In their statements the women never
mention thunderbolts or the raw cunning
of all those disguises. Reading the column
inches, I thought it smacked of raging
entitlement and the rather prosaic urge
to get one over on many-eyed Hera.
A swan. A bull. An ant. An eagle.
A flame. A goddamn shower of gold.
Actress/model/nymph. Eighty-seven of them.
The women brave enough to tumble a god.
The only common features were the bathrobe
and the titan weight of his threats.
He may be in prison, but Olympus still stands,
the letters tall and white on the Hollywood hills.
Another colossus naked beneath the robe, dusting off
the casting couch, rearranging the pot-plants.

Bios

Jude Aquilina lives in the lakeside town of Milang where she works as a freelance writer, teacher and editor. Jude has published poetry, short fiction and non-fiction across Australia and abroad. She was awarded the Barbara Hanrahan Fellowship in 2018, for sustained contribution to South Australian Literature. Jude gives thanks to women writers who've been inspiring role models, such as Gwen Harwood, Judith Wright, Isabel Allende, Lorna Crozier and Jan Owen.

Lin Blythe is a proud Eurasian woman, socialist activist and lover of speculative fiction. The biggest influences on her writing, who also happen to be her favourite authors, are Ursula K Le Guin, Alice Pung, Ray Bradbury, Ibram X Kendi, Alastair Reynolds, Ken Liu, Martha Wells and Aliette De Boddard. To her, stories are both an escape from the world and a catalyst for progress in the world. Often, Lin finds herself writing about her family's intergenerational trauma, space and vampires. Her essays, short fiction and poetry have been published in Overland, the UTS 2022 Anthology: Turn Left on Red Permitted After Stopping and the Moon Orchard (2022) audiobook.

Arielle Bodenstein is often creating fake scenarios in her head. A Google search diagnosed the condition as 'maladaptive daydreaming', which she thinks is a surprisingly accurate description of what it's like to be a writer. Her stories seek out the poetic potential of the everyday, showcased through simple narratives about complex emotions.

Alisha Brown is a queer poet living on unceded Yuin country. She placed second in the Judith Rodriguez Open Section of the 2021 Woorilla Poetry Prize and was shortlisted for the SCWC 2022 Poetry Award. You can find her words in the Australian Poetry Anthology Vol 9, Fine Print Magazine, Baby Teeth Journal,

Aniko Magazine, Art Collector Magazine, and the South Coast Writers' Centre anthology, Legacies.

Natalie Damjanovich-Napoleon (D-Napoleon) is a writer and singer-songwriter from Fremantle, Australia. She spent the last decade in the United States where she worked as a Coordinator at a City College Writing Centre. Her work has appeared in Meanjin, The Manifest-Station, Cordite, Found Poetry Review, Australian Poetry Journal and Writer's Digest (US). Recently, she was an International Guest of the Perth Poetry Festival. Her poem "First Blood: A Sestina" won the prestigious Bruce Dawe Poetry Prize (2018) through the University of Southern Queensland. In 2019 Ginninderra Press released D-Napoleon's debut poetry collection First Blood. In 2021 Natalie completed her second poetry collection on motherhood, the silencing of women's voices and the power of the unknown. Currently Natalie is teaching writing at ECU while completing a PhD on erasure poetry and historic amnesia.

Emma Darcy has a degree in Creative Writing and a Masters in Museum and Heritage Studies. She works as a digital archivist and library assistant. She has always been fascinated by folklore and myth, but typically writes horror. Emma has two children with her wife, Mandy, her high school sweetheart. 'Return to the Labyrinth' is her first published short story.

Rachel Flynn is best known for her picture books and novels for children, some of which have been translated into French, Spanish, Dutch, Chinese, Korean and Turkish. Her most widely read novel is *Sacked*, in which Edward sacks his mother for not doing her mothering job to his requirements. Rachel is also an occasional poet with work ranging from cultural commentary to interpretations of weather and landscape. Short fiction is a regular creative outlet. *Jeff and Jill* won first prize in the Sutherland Shire Literary Competition in 2020 and *Honey* was shortlisted in the Peter Carey Short Story Award, 2022. Rachel's writing explores themes of balance and imbalance between adults and children, men and women, different generations, and between the recent past and the present. She has just completed a PhD in creative writing.

Jane Frank's latest chapbook is *Wide River* (Calanthe Press, 2020). Her poems have won awards and been widely published both in Australia and internationally, appearing most recently in Westerly, Plumwood Mountain, StylusLit, Poetry Ireland Review and a number of anthologies including Poetry for the Planet, The Incompleteness Book II, The Newcastle Poetry Prize Anthology 2021 and Not Very Quiet: The Anthology. Originally from the Fraser Coast, Jane lives in Brisbane and teaches in humanities at Griffith University.

Dr Verity Laughton is an Adelaide-based poet and playwright of more than 30 plays and other works. Her work has been produced locally, nationally, and internationally. She completed a PhD in political theatre at Flinders University in 2020. For this she wrote a new play, the epic scaled Zosia's Story. Recent full-length works are the verbatim theatre piece Long Tan (Brink Production, 2017), and The Red Cross Letters (STCSA, 2016). Her works have been published by Currency Press, Phoenix Educational/Five Senses Press, Federation Press, Omnibus Press, and others. Awards include AWGIES for Radio Drama and Community, the Inscription Open Award, SA Critics' Circle Best New Play Award and the Griffin Prize. Current work includes the adaptation of a major Australian contemporary novel for the State Theatre Company of South Australia (2023) and a poetry collection, Snake, for The Signalhouse Edition (also 2023). She is a member of the playwrights' group, 7-ON. www.veritylaughton.com

Wes Lee lives in New Zealand. Her latest poetry collection, By the Lapels, was launched in 2019 (Steele Roberts Aotearoa). She has won a number of awards for her writing including The BNZ Katherine Mansfield Literary Award, and The Bronwyn Tate

Memorial Award. Most recently she was awarded the Poetry New Zealand Prize 2019 by Massey University Press, and shortlisted for The NZSA Laura Solomon Cuba Press Prize 2022. Her work has appeared in a wide array of literary journals and anthologies in New Zealand, Australia and the UK, including Best New Zealand Poems, Southword, The North, Westerly, Cordite, Landfall, Poetry London, New Writing Scotland, The London Magazine, The Stinging Fly, Silence: The University of Canberra Vice-Chancellor's Poetry Prize Anthology 2019, The New Zealand Listener, Australian Poetry Journal.

Rachael Mead is a South Australian novelist and poet, with her creative work appearing widely in Australia and internationally. She's the author of the novel 'The Application of Pressure' (Affirm Press 2020) and four collections of poetry including 'The Flaw in the Pattern' (UWAP 2018). In 2022, she won the Barbara Hanrahan Fellowship in the Adelaide Festival Awards for Literature to continue work on her novel about the first Australian woman in Antarctica.

Sara C. Motta is a proud Mestiza-salvaje of Colombia-Chibcha/Muisca, Eastern European Jewish and Celtic linages currently living, loving and re-existiendo on the unceded lands of the Awabakal and Worimi peoples, NSW, so called Australia. She is mother, survivor of state and intimate violences, poet, curandera, bare-breasted philosopher, popular educator, and Associate Professor at the University of Newcastle, NSW. Sara has worked for over two decades with raced and feminised communities in struggle resistances/re-existencias in, against and beyond heteronormative capitalist-coloniality in Europe, Latin America and Australia and co-created numerous decolonising pedagogical projects of radical healing and community wellbeing. She has published widely in academic and activist-community outlets. Her latest book Liminal Subjects: Weaving (Our) Liberation (Rowman and Littlefield) is winner of the 2020 best

Gender Theory and Feminist Book, International Studies Associate (ISA).

Kerry Munnery is a writer who likes to explore the boundaries where what is familiar and known nudges against the unsettled and uncanny. Her short stories have been placed in or won various competitions including the Neilma Sidney, the Grace Marion Wilson, and the Newcastle Short Story Awards. She has also published creative non-fiction and children's fiction. She has a Masters of Arts by Research in Creative Writing from RMIT, and lives and works in Melbourne, on the lands of the Wurundjeri people.

Jan Napier is a Western Australian writer. Her villanelle Wiltshire 1840 won the Ethel Webb Blundell Poetry Prize 2022. Jan's first poetry collection Thylacine was launched in 2015. Both her second collection Day Moon (haiku), and third collection Listening to Frost were published in 2020. Jan's work has been showcased in journals and anthologies both within Australia and overseas.

Emily Paskevics divides her time between Toronto and northwestern Ontario, Canada. Her short fiction has appeared in The Hopper & the Humber Literary Review, among others. She is a 2022 finalist for the Bronwen Wallace Award for Emerging Writers, via the Writers Trust of Canada. She was also longlisted for the 2019 CBC Short Story Prize. She is a graduate of the Humber School for Writers, in Toronto. Find her online at @epaskev and https://linktr.ee/epaskev.

Kathryn Reese is a writer and poet living in Adelaide. Kathryn is passionate about collaborative process and facilitates workshops that teach participants to settle anxiety and access their creativity. Her writing explores themes of nature, spirituality, myth and the possibility of shape shift. Her poetry collection "Despair Dragon:

notes on survival" was written amongst the chaos of parenting and trauma, finding hope and connection in unexpected ways.

Brittany Riley is a writer from country NSW who tinkers in fiction, screenwriting, and poetry. She self-published her YA fantasy novel at 22, and currently works for a national children's poetry competition. When she's not writing, she's thinking about writing, drinking far too much coffee, or giggling at cat videos. This is her first anthology feature.

Paris Rosemont is a poet with a passion for the arts. She has crafted award-winning poetry that has been described as 'edgy confessional' and 'visceral hyperrealism'. Paris' poetry was selected by Red Room Poetry for publication in Upswell Publishing's anthology 'Admissions', alongside established writers, musicians and notable public figures. Having received a scholarship to study at the Australian Theatre for Young People, Paris combines her love for poetry and theatre into the exploration of the art of performance poetry. She has performed her poetry to live audiences in venues ranging from Sappho Books to West Side Slam to Sydney University's Chau Chak Wing Museum. Paris was the first poet invited to perform a solo set of her original poetry at Rhapsody Revue and is a swing poet for the Sydney Fringe Festival 2022. Paris was a judge for the Living Stories Writing Competition 2022. She is also a WestWords 2022 Academian and a Frontier Poetry scholarship recipient.

Janeen Samuel is a former veterinary pathologist who lives in South-West Victoria, surrounded by sheep and slumbering volcanoes. Her poems and short fiction have been published in, among others: Andromeda Spaceways Inflight Magazine; Award Winning Australian Writing (Melbourne Books); the speculative poetry anthology The Stars Like Sand (Interactive Press, Brisbane 2014); Cicerone on-line journal, 2020; and Crossed Spaces (Rhiza Edge, 2021), an anthology for young adults.

Kathryn Simons is a South Australian writer of Fantasy. She wrote her Honours thesis on revisionary feminist mythmaking and explores similar themes in her fiction through rewriting Polish and Latvian folklore.

Alicia Sometimes is a poet and broadcaster. She has performed her spoken word and poetry at many venues, festivals and events around the world. She is director and co-writer of the science-poetry planetarium shows, Elemental and Particle/Wave. Her TedxUQ talk in 2019 was about combining art with science. She is currently a Science Gallery Melbourne 'Leonardo' (creative advisor). In 2021 she completed the Boyd Garret residency for the City of Melbourne and a Virtual Writer in Residency for Manchester City of Literature and Manchester Literature Festival.

Beth Spencer writes a mix of fiction, poetry, memoir and essay. Her most recent book is The Age of Fibs: stories, memoir, microlit (Spineless Wonders, 2022). Others include How to Conceive for a Girl (Random House) which was runner up for the Steele Rudd Award, and Vagabondage, a poetry memoir about a year living in a campervan (UWAP). She has won several prizes and awards and her work has been supported by the Literature Board and CreateNSW. She lives on Guringai land on the Central Coast, NSW, and at www.bethspencer.com.

Kyla St Jaye is Mparntwe based (Alice Springs NT), writing from Arrernte country. She studied creative writing on Ngunnawal country at University of Canberra where she won an ACT writers centre award and was featured in several publications. Kyla took this practice into the women's refuges on Yuin country (Far South Coast, NSW) where she facilitated many writing programs and group publications under a narrative therapy framework. Her programs recognised stories as transformative power sites for women who had experienced trauma, homelessness and domestic violence. They used creative practice to position women as the authors of their own lives. She currently works these programs online, looks after her children and writes in the red dirt.

Sarah Temporal is a prize-winning poet, writer and educator from the Northern Rivers NSW. She began her journey with spoken-word in the early 2000s as part of Australia's first slam poetry team, and has since performed at festivals and events Australia-wide. More recently her work has been published in Best of Australian Poems and Alphabet of Women, and twice shortlisted for the XYZ Prize for Innovation in Spoken-Word. Sarah now works to empower voices of all ages through her regional arts initiative, Poets Out Loud. She collaborates with circus artist Britt Portelli on 'The Birth Suite', a performance project exploring transition, birth and motherhood.

Clare Testoni is a playwright, fiction writer, and puppeteer. Resent performed works include The Secret Garden, Tale of Tales, The Double, and the children's radio-play SunRunners. Clare won the AAWP/ASSF Emerging Writers' Short Story Prize in 2021 and has been published in Westerly, UNSWeetened, and in the anthology South of The Sun: Australian Fairy Tales for the 21st century. Originally from Sydney, she currently lives in Fremantle, Western Australia and is a PhD candidate in creative writing at The University of Western Australia.

Emily Tsokos Purtill is a Western Australian writer of Greek heritage. She has lived in Shropshire, London, Vancouver, Paris and most recently, New York City. Emily's creative non-fiction, short fiction, flash fiction and poetry has been published in anthologies and journals in Australia and the United States. In 2020 Emily was shortlisted for the ACU Prize for Poetry.

Romy Tara Wenzel is a writer and artist on Melukerdee country, Tasmania, exploring mythology and ecology from an animist perspective. Recent publications include stories in Dark Mountain, Cunning Folk and House of Twigs. Her work has been shortlisted for several prizes including the Tasmanian Writers' Prize and the Speculate Prize. Instagram @the_quiet_wilds

Editor, **Sarah Nicholson** is the creative director of The Heroines Festival and editor of the Heroines Anthology. She is an academic and writer who teaches in literature, philosophy, creative arts, gender and religious studies. She is a past director of the National Young Writers' Festival, awardee of the Ian Potter Cultural Trust for Literature, and recipient of a Writer's and Translator's Centre of Rhodes fellowship. She was the 2017 Emerging Writer in Residence for the Katherine Susannah Pritchard Writers' Centre. She is the author of *The Evolutionary Journey of Woman* and an editor of *Integral Voices on Sex, Gender and Sexuality*. She is the chair of board of the South Coast Writers' Centre, and also the founder of The Neo Perennial Press, established as part of Wollongong Council's Creative Spaces program.

Co-editor, **Lore White** is the editor of *Baby Teeth Journal*, as well as a freelance copywriter and blogger.

www.ingramcontent.com/pod-product-compliance
Lightning Source LLC
Chambersburg PA
CBHW071006120726
47910CB00004B/1409